THE VOYAGE OF
THE ASTEROID

By
LAURENCE MANNING

ARMCHAIR FICTION
PO Box 4369, Medford, Oregon 97504

THEY WERE FIRST TO SET FOOT ON VENUS

When Haworth invited Mason and Bigelow to join him for a trip of indefinite duration, a trip that promised plenty of excitement and danger, too, they thought he was referring to a destination somewhere on the planet Earth. But when he showed them his huge rocket ship—a mighty vehicle it had taken him years to build—they could hardly contain their excitement. Space!

Their destination was to be Earth's nearest planetary neighbor—the far-off, cloud-shrouded planet of Venus. So it was with the greatest anticipation that Haworth and his friends boarded his spacecraft, "The Asteroid," and blasted off into the void of deep space. But they could have hardly anticipated the planet they landed on—a fog-covered world filled with bizarre vegetation, foul smelling air, gigantic prehistoric beasts, and a strange, but intelligent race of club-wielding lizard-men. It soon became apparent to the three explorers from Earth that their safe return home was anything but guaranteed.

FOR A SECOND NOVEL, TURN TO PAGE 135

ABOUT LAURENCE MANNING...

Laurence Manning was born July 20th, 1899 in St John, New Brunswick and attended Kings College in Halifax, Nova Scotia. In 1920 he moved to the United States and became a U.S. citizen. He lived primarily on Staten Island, where he began writing short stories for several pulp science fiction magazines.

Manning was a founding member of the American Rocket Society, serving as both president and editor. For his involvement in the Society, Manning was recognized by the Smithsonian's National Air and Space Museum as an early rocketry pioneer. Manning retired from the American Rocket Society in the mid-1940s, stating that rocketry had 'grown up', and was no longer a place for amateurs. In 1961, Manning was awarded a lifetime membership in the Society, that award being presented by then Vice President Lyndon B. Johnson.

Manning had given up his successful writing career at the end of 1935 and devoted his time to a mail order nursery business he owned and managed. Apart from a few short stories in the 1950s, he never penned any further works of science fiction. However, he was the author of a successful book on gardening, *The How and Why of Better Gardening* (1951). Manning had three children: Helen Louise, Dorothy, and James Edward. He lived in Highlands, New Jersey from 1951 until his death on April 10th, 1972.

CHAPTER ONE
The Strange Flying Machine

I WOULD have forgotten what day it was except for Mason. He solemnly entered my bedroom that morning, bearing a loaf of pound cake into which he had stuck three dozen candles. It made a sorry mess, the more so when he had lit the tapers and the wax dripped an unwholesome pink icing over all.

"Thirty-six years old," he pronounced, brooding over his gift. "You are very nicely divisible by three and two in all their combinations. Last year it was five and seven and a little more unusual. But thirty-six is a very practical number in many ways—how does it feel?"

This curse of absurd humor is, in my opinion, one reason that Dr. Arthur Finch Mason is still only an associate professor of mathematics. He was inordinately popular with his students and he was very successful in instilling in them not only a knowledge of his subject but a sincere liking for it as well. But he achieved his results only after breaking half the rules of pedagogy and his fellow members on the faculty observed his progress with some distrust.

We had been at college together—close friends, in fact. Three years ago he had come to me in deep distress, for his young wife had died and he was once more alone in the world. We had obtained an apartment in West 86th street and moved in as permanent partners. Living in New York can be a lonely business and I found Mason an ideal companion—sensible and earnest beneath his camouflage of absurdity. Physically he was tall and thin, with pale and rather distinguished features. His demeanor was serious and dignified, a fact which rendered his drolleries all the more remarkable and—to some extent—incomprehensible.

"Now next year," continued my friend, "you will have reached a prime number—thirty-seven. I wonder whether a man is in his prime only when his age is? There's an idea! The prime ages of man—at one the puling infant; at three the walking, talking terror!"

I was not in the mood for nonsense that morning and proceeded to the bathroom for a shower. Mason was tenacious, however, and followed me in. Over the noise of the shower I could hear him continuing his witticism to its bitter end.

"Seven is the age of first sense and schooling; eleven and thirteen arrive with puberty…"

I turned the water on full force and drowned out his voice. But when I had finished bathing and proceeded to get dressed he was still at it.

"Thirty-seven," he was saying, "is the prime of life. From then the mainspring commences to unwind. This year, Bigelow, is your last year of youth!"

Breakfast silenced him at last. This particular morning was a Saturday and neither of us was compelled to labor. We settled down to a day of rest. I browsed through a copy of *Lens and Bellows*—one magazine of which I am editor—and mused idly upon certain changes I had in mind for the next issue. But my mind refused to remain engaged upon the print before me. I found myself in a sober, thoughtful mood. Mason's mock seriousness had had its effect on me.

Thirty-six years old, I thought. Rather soon now it would be forty, then fifty. Then what? Was I really doing the kind of thing I wanted to do with my life? My memory conjured up myself at twenty—a budding young naturalist full of purpose and courage. Once I had other plans for my career:

adventurous expeditions to out-of-the-way lands looking for strange plants and animals—the thrill of discovery! The heady wine of fame! But here I was and here was I likely to remain until I died. I could see the obituary notices of my death. They would be tucked away on inside pages of newspapers. My own magazine would give a history of my life in a black-bordered page. Then oblivion.

I sighed and stirred restlessly in the comfortable lounge chair.

"What's the use of it all?" I exclaimed aloud.

Mason looked up from his book. "There is an unwritten law against philosophy before noon. What you need is some exercise. Fresh air! A glimpse of life and motion! Let's go for a drive."

"Where to?" I queried listlessly.

"The Connecticut countryside should be worth a look this time of year. Evergreens will be budding out—maples coming into leaf. There are a thousand things to see."

"All right, I'll take along a camera."

Mason raised his eyebrows humorously. "Of course! How could I have forgotten that detail?"

We donned hats and coats and walked around to the garage and started up Riverside Drive. Thus casually commenced the series of events that led to the greatest adventure of our lives. There is an extraordinary orderliness about life. One little thing compels another to follow it, until the ultimate happening is inevitable.

The country was beautiful. We went up through Westchester County and inland across the state line into Connecticut. Mason drove. Now and again we stopped while I took a picture and a little after one o'clock we had lunch on sandwiches and beer at a roadside stand.

I took the wheel after that and, following the mood of the moment, turned into a side road and went for some miles along it. Again I took an inviting branch road and proceeded without thought or care for direction or destination until we found ourselves bumping along parallel ruts in a single-track lane that wound in and about hedges of cat-vine and alder.

The spring sun brought out the fragrance of the leaves and flowers and we stopped the car and climbed out. I was setting up the camera in this idyllic scene when it happened— a sudden hissing roar passed from right to left overhead and I caught a glimpse of a round dark thing flashing higher and higher until it disappeared in the sky.

I turned to Mason, who was still staring with open mouth.

"What in Heaven's name was that?"

Mason stared without reply at the spot where it had vanished. Suddenly I heard him gasp. I looked up eagerly. There was an airplane descending swiftly toward us. Its motor was evidently shut off, for it made no sound. It soared overhead not five hundred feet up and seemed to be aiming for the ground just beyond the hedgerow on our right. We had a brief view of it, and strange enough it seemed. The wings were unusually short and stubby. The fuselage was enormous in proportion—perhaps fifty feet across and as much long. It was shaped like a cylinder and was dull silver in color. There did not seem to be any landing wheels.

"Come on!" Mason burst excitedly through the hedge and disappeared from view. I followed, tearing my clothes on the thorns of the cat-vine, but thinking nothing of it. We ran for five minutes up a slight slope of shrubs and weeds and were stopped by a stone wall. It was no ordinary Connecticut dry rubble wall, but rose twelve feet high and was well cemented. Trees made a thicket, which concealed its existence until we were within a few feet of the obstruction.

"Now what?" I panted.

"OVER it!" answered Mason and with the agility of a boy he commenced to climb a tree whose branches brushed the top of the wall. We managed to climb along these branches and reach the jagged top without mishap. But our view was not better in the least. Beyond the wall we found that the ground rose, heavily wooded. It was a scene of some charm and beauty, but our curiosity was too much aroused to permit our enjoying it.

"There doesn't seem to be anyone in sight," remarked Mason thoughtfully.

"It would be trespassing," I demurred.

"I'm going down," he announced determinedly.

And down we went, hanging by our fingers and dropping to the earth beneath. We pushed our way stealthily uphill through the woods for five minutes—like schoolboys on an apple raid. I began to realize the awkwardness of our position.

"I'm going back, Mason! Suppose we're caught here—rather embarrassing for us, don't you think? It was just an airplane, anyway."

"No airplane ever went as fast as that. I've simply got to see what it was. Come on, Bigelow! Nobody will see us. Let's go to the top of this hill at least. Perhaps we can see from there."

In a few moments we did indeed reach the top of the hill and the edge of the woods at the same time. The ground dropped away before us in a slope perhaps a half mile long. Rock and grass shared this incline and at the foot a broad meadow country led the eye to wooded hills some two miles beyond. We looked down into a completely enclosed valley.

A lake lay in the meadowland. It was some miles in length and half that in width. On the far side stood a tall building of peculiar shape. Partly pulled up on the shore lay our airplane—if it was one. Even at that distance we could make out the figures of men around it and presently a huge derrick swung out from the side of the building and the strange ship began to crawl slowly farther up the shore. We were at a loss for an explanation of anything we saw. I was just going to speak to Mason when a crisp voice startled me:

"Put them up!"

We swung around and gazed guiltily at a very large revolver. Holding it was a short, sturdy person, very red of face. He was dressed in brown knee breeches and leather leggings. A rough khaki shirt and peaked cap completed his attire. Red-faced ourselves, we put our hands in the air.

He pointed along the crest of the hill to the left.

"March!" he ordered.

We obeyed. A faint path was marked through the brush and this we followed for not more than a hundred yards when the wall came again into sight. A grilled iron gate was let into it at this point. Our captor commanded us to unlatch it. We did so and passed through, whereupon he closed and locked the gate behind us.

We stood on the roadway feeling (for my own part) decidedly foolish. Our late captor eyed us phlegmatically through the grill.

"What is this place?" demanded Mason.

He received no answer and I could see his cheek flush with anger.

"Who owns it?" I queried impatiently.

"You'd best move on," said the man in brown. "I've no information to give out."

I was quite irritated. "My good man," I said firmly, "we are respectable men and have asked you civil questions. Whatever your orders may be, they do not include incivility to strangers, I am sure."

His grin made me more annoyed than ever. With a senseless desire to impress the man, I fumbled for my card case and handed a card through the gate.

"If you will be so good as to give that to your master," I requested with what I hoped was biting dignity, "and explain to him that we saw his airplane and followed its course out of natural curiosity. I will give you a dollar."

"Oh all right!" he said curtly, "'Twill do you no good though."

I handed in the dollar and we walked in silence back to the car. Mason drove at a vicious pace and we soon came out upon a well-surfaced road. We found ourselves only seven miles from Silvermine, according to the signpost. Being so close to the seacoast, we kept our course along various roads leading southeast until we reached the Boston Post Road, and thence back to New York. It was evening when we reached our apartment.

"What did you give that fool your card for?" growled Mason.

"It was the proper thing to do," I answered, flushing slightly at the memory. "I wish I knew who the brute is!"

Mason grunted and proceeded to disrobe. He entered the bathroom and I heard the shower running. I was in no mood for sleep. The events of the day had somehow I turned my mind back fifteen years. A great discontent possessed me. I rooted about in the bottom of my trunk and brought to light my notes on paleobotany. I turned the pages moodily, surprised to find that my work had been rather good. Some photographs of specimens were pasted in the pages of the notebook to remind me of my one summer of unalloyed joy, collecting fossil plants in Montana.

Mason came into the room clad in his bathrobe.

"Some people have all the luck," he said. "Think of owning a hidden valley in Connecticut and having nothing to do but experiment with flying machines!"

He sighed. "Do you know," he added, "I'm going to take my sabbatical year starting this summer. I'm getting bored with all this."

"Where will you go?" I asked enviously.

"I think I can get Perkins to let me in at the Mount Wilson Observatory. He's going to work on spectroscopic analyses of the planets next year. It should be fun, I've always been interested in the subject."

"Curious you should mention your astronomy! I have just been thinking about my own hobby—looking up my notes on paleobotany."

Mason nodded soberly. "What we both need is some excitement," he said.

IT was, I believe, on the next Wednesday that a series of small mysterious events commenced. I had just returned to my office after lunch when Jackson, my assistant, told me that I had had a caller during my absence.

"Said he was from the Mutual Insurance Company," offered Jackson. "Asked for you, but when I told him you were out he said it didn't matter. All he wanted was to find out if you really worked here. Matter of form, I took it. Checking up for that new policy you are taking out with his company, you know."

"But Jackson! I am not taking out an insurance policy with the Mutual or any other company!"

Jackson looked surprised.

"Must have been someone else then…but he seemed to be certain of your name. Stephen Bigelow, he said."

I inquired as to what sort of things he wanted to know. Apparently he had confined his questions to my business connections.

"Oh yes," added Jackson, "he asked if you kept mostly in the office or went out-of-doors a good deal. Seemed to think you were a botanist."

"What did he look like?"

But my assistant only remembered that he had been rather short and slight. "Pleasant sod of fellow, you know."

I dismissed the matter from my mind until I got back to the apartment that evening. Sam, the elevator boy, spoke to me.

"There was a man askin' about you here today, suh."

"What did he want, Sam?"

"Just wanted to make sure you-all lived here, I reckon. Said he was from a department store, Mister Bigelow."

Mason was in the apartment when I opened the door. I told him and he was as mystified as I.

"I have no account with any department store, Mason, and I am taking out no insurance. What do you suppose is going on?"

And the next evening when I got home after work Mason informed me that our mysterious and indefatigable questioner had been up at the University asking about him!

"You don't suppose," I suggested hesitantly, "that it has anything to do with my giving my name up in Connecticut Saturday?"

"Why on earth should it? Besides, that would be only *your* name. Why should anyone poke his nose into my affairs? I didn't leave any fool card!"

"Well, perhaps he got your name from Sam at the elevator when he called yesterday," I hazarded.

Mason smiled. "Come!" he said, brightening visibly. "Here we are saying 'perhaps' to things! Well—perhaps, then! Perhaps it's all a deep-laid plot of Italian racketeers. Tired of robbing restaurants and fruit stands, they are going to levy tribute on all salaried men! Ten percent of our income—or they bump us off in some unusual and mysterious way!"

"For Heaven's sake, Mason! Can't you be serious?"

"Perhaps you are really heir to an Earldom and the solicitors are making prudent investigations into your habits before…"

But I put my fingers to my ears and commenced reading a book with exaggerated concentration.

Friday night we had a visitor. Mason and I were quietly reading when the doorbell rang. I answered it and in the hall outside stood a rather tall, well-dressed man. His face was shrouded in black whiskers and a well-trimmed beard tapered to his chest.

"Does Mr. Stephen Bigelow live here?" he asked in a deep bass voice.

"I am Mr. Bigelow," I replied.

My visitor stared doubtfully in the half-light of the vestibule. "Why, I believe you are Bigelow!" he exclaimed. "Do you remember me? I'm Haworth—used to know you at Columbia."

It was my turn to stare, for his beard was a thorough disguise. Certainly there was something familiar about the man. "Come in," I invited. "I certainly remember Haworth—but I can't say as much for his beard."

"I had completely forgotten. Of course you wouldn't recognize me this way," he said apologetically as he entered. He stared a moment at my friend. "Why it is…isn't this Mason?" he exclaimed.

"It is," I replied and they shook hands cordially. Mason had known Haworth rather better than I, and seemed to recognize him in spite of changes.

Haworth explained his presence, "Happened to be in town tonight with nothing to do. I thought I remembered that Bigelow lived in New York, so I looked him up in the phone book, found his address and dropped over. I'm staying at the Grandison just up the street a block. Fancy my finding Mason here as well," he exclaimed. "How are the mathematics?"

We talked for some time about other days. I had to explain that biology—while still my hobby—had not continued to be my sole work in the world.

"Curious that photography—a mere side line to my original life-work—should not provide me with a living," I said.

But Haworth was much interested in photography, it appeared, and nothing would do but he must see some of my pictures.

And Mason's astronomical leanings were duly recollected and his plans for a year at the observatory on Mount Wilson outlined.

"How are you on navigation, Mason?" asked Haworth suddenly.

We both looked at him in surprise. He seemed embarrassed and muttered some words into his beard.

"To tell the truth," he explained, "I am planning a trip to...to some out-of-the-way parts this coming year. Er...ah...part of the way by air." He seemed to be choosing his words with great care. "I need a good navigator. Not only that, but a man I can trust as a traveling companion as well. I thought perhaps...well, if you weren't absolutely settled on going to the Coast next year..."

His voice trailed off ineffectually.

Mason puffed quietly at his pipe.

"I don't know. What sort of a trip is it going to be?"

"Scientific exploration," replied Haworth. "As a matter of fact, I could use a naturalist, too. Particularly if he were handy with a camera." He turned to me. "It would be absolutely ideal if we could all three go along. Now if you could drop your magazine for a year, Bigelow, we could..."

"Just a moment, Haworth!" I interrupted. "How did you know I worked on a magazine?"

"Oh damn!" he replied. He seemed to think a minute and then shrugged his shoulders. "I might have known I couldn't carry it through. Never was any good at this sort of thing. I'll have to make a clean breast of it."

"You certainly will!" And I strode over to stand between him and the door by which he had entered.

CHAPTER TWO
Haworth's Proposal

HE looked at me quizzically. "Oh, it's nothing much to tell," he said. "You needn't get excited. One of my men caught you nosing around at my place last Saturday."

Mason rose excitedly. "So you're the man! What on earth kind of flying machine have you got there? Why are you so secretive about it?"

"And why have you been putting detectives upon us?" I added.

"One at a time! One at a time!" replied our visitor. "I'm not going to say just now what kind of a vessel I've been building. But I really am going on a trip in her and I am really looking for two men to go with me. Curiously enough, you two are exactly qualified—made to order for the job! That's why I came to look you over and make your acquaintance again. I see you haven't changed much since the old days— men sometimes do, you know.

"When Jones brought me your card, Bigelow, I was just on the point of writing our old professor to see if he could recommend anyone for the post. But I remembered you had been trained as a naturalist and I wrote a detective agency to look you up. As soon as I got a report from them that you were living with Mason—well, here I am."

He peered at us shrewdly. "Come, what do you say? A trip of indefinite duration. Plenty of excitement and plenty of danger, too, I must admit. But there's a chance, if we succeed, to make yourselves famous from one end of the world to the other. There will be enough new material to make a dozen scientific treatises. We won't fail for lack of capital, that I can assure you. My people left me well off—I've more money than I can spend, as a matter of fact. But I'll spend every cent of it if need be."

"That's all very well, Haworth," I said. "But where are you going? You can't expect us to start off with you like this. Speaking for myself, at least, I should want to see your airplane and study your plans most carefully before I pretended to make any decision whatsoever."

"And so you shall," said Haworth, nodding his head decisively so that his beard raised and lowered itself on his chest. "The ship's sound enough, you'll find. And as for our destination, I would even go so far as to take your advice in the matter, Mason. What I really want to know tonight is whether, all other things being satisfactory, you would consider such an adventure? How about you?"

"Hmmm! X being unknown and Y not given, find their respective values!" replied Mason thoughtfully. "It's quite a pig-in-a-poke business, Haworth. But if it proves interesting—of course—I'd be interested, wouldn't I. I'd go, that is, provided Bigelow would go along, too. How about it, old man?"

The whole suggestion was so unusual and irregular that I could not master a rising irritation.

"What an absurd way to propose a scientific expedition! If you mean to ask us whether we could go if we wanted to, I can only say, of course we could. Someone else could take over my work. I presume some remuneration would be provided, Haworth?"

He nodded emphatically, without speaking.

"Why don't you tell us frankly what kind of a trip you have in mind?" I burst forth. "I don't like this air of mystery at all."

"Neither do I, Bigelow," was the surprising rejoinder. "This is no usual trip I plan. I have found it does not pay to talk about it. Some have seen fit to ridicule it and so I'm trying to keep it quiet until plans are farther along. Then too, I will have certain inventions to put through the Patent Office. I'll agree to this much, however. Sleep on it tonight. Tomorrow we'll have lunch together at the Grandison and if you can say that you are honestly interested—no more than that—I'll tell you the whole story and you can make a definite decision."

And since he gathered up his hat and cane at this point, and bade us a determined good night, we had to be contented with that.

Next morning I awoke early and lay quietly in bed, felt, for some unknown reason, that I should be happy and excited about something. It was several minutes before I remembered the events of the previous evening and I was suddenly thrilled and interested. I glanced at my bedside alarm clock and, since it read only eight o'clock. I did not rise—although I was by now thoroughly awake...

Saturday morning once more, I thought, and nothing in particular to do. Our appointment with Haworth was for lunch. My thoughts went back the long vista of Saturday mornings I had spent in this apartment and the drab comfort of it seemed, for no good reason, quite unalluring. I analyzed my feelings and came to realize just how dulled and bored my senses had been for months past. I made up my mind then and there that if Haworth's proposal moved in any way a sensible one that I should certainly accept it. What kind of a trip, I thought, would require an airplane such as we had seen last week? Possibly, it occurred to me, some very inaccessible country like...like the country of the Amazon, for instance. Perhaps that was where Haworth proposed exploring. I was on the point of rising to suggest this to Mason, when he appeared, yawning, in my doorway.

"Half past eight," he announced. "How do you feel about Haworth this morning?"

"What do you know about him?" I countered.

Mason frowned sleepily. "You remember him at college? Well, let's see now. You were there that night he left. Poor chap! His father was Haworth of the Haworth Silk millions. Left it all behind him when he was killed that night. Charlie Haworth was the only son. I haven't heard anything about him for years, so I don't know any more than you what he has been up to, but at college, he majored in physics and astronomy. He had some rather sound theories on general science and some fairly wild ones on political economy. Rather a steady chap, I'd say, and persistent. Obstinate, in fact. But he's a good sort and should have both the necessary brains and money to getup something real in the way of an exploring trip."

I ASKED Mason what he thought of the possibility that Haworth's goal might be the Amazon River country and we soon had an Atlas out on the table measuring distances and reckoning probable courses. By ten o'clock we sat down to breakfast half persuaded that we had guessed the purpose of the voyage. We need not be criticized for this, since there is a vast area absolutely unexplored and unattainable by ordinary means of travel.

Time dragged slowly that morning. At twelve o'clock we dressed and departed, being unable to wait longer. I found myself full of overpowering curiosity and eagerness. At the Grandison, Haworth sent down word to wait in the lobby and, fortunately for our patience, which was fast departing, he arrived a few minutes after we had received his message.

"Well?" he asked.

Mason looked at me and I nodded determinedly. "We will probably go with you," I said. "Now tell us what it's all about!"

But Haworth seemed unwilling to do this immediately and I found some of the annoyance and suspicion of last night returning to me.

"Let us have our lunch first," he demurred. "I'm hungry. We will have all the rest of the day, you know."

I cannot now recall anything that I ate that meal. Possibly I never knew. Somehow it was finished and our cigarettes were alight.

"You know, Haworth, we've guessed pretty well where you are going, anyway!"

He looked up, startled.

Mason nodded his head sagaciously. "It's the Amazon River, isn't it?"

Haworth colored slightly. His hand fingered his beard nervously. "Not exactly," he replied. "That ought to be done sometime, of course, but I am planning a more interesting trip than that by long odds."

He reached into his pocket and produced a photographic print.

"Look this over," he said, and I thought he seemed embarrassed.

Mason and I put our heads together over the photograph. It was seemingly a white ball set in a black background. The plate was foggy and the picture not a very clear one. There seemed no purpose in showing it to us.

I looked up inquiringly.

"Look closely at it," urged Haworth.

And I did. The white ball was the Earth. There, faintly marked on its surface, were the continents of North and South America, slightly obscured by patches of vague gray.

"Good Lord!" exploded Mason.

"Exactly," observed Haworth and puffed a cloud of smoke contentedly toward the ceiling.

But I was just beginning to realize the implications. "Do you mean to say," I began, "that this photograph…"

Haworth held up his hand and I stopped. "That photograph was taken by me with a small Kodak two months ago."

"Then where were you?" I asked in bewilderment.

"About two thousand miles above the earth!"

"Not in the ship we saw? Of course! Of course!" exclaimed Mason.

"The same. Some slight changes had been made when you saw it, but substantially the same ship," replied our host.

"But man alive!" shouted Mason, forgetting our surroundings entirely. "Then our expedition…is going to be… Great Heavens!"

"Exactly!" nodded Charles Haworth. "Great Heavens! And wherever in them we want to voyage."

We need not have been as startled as we were. After all, Professor Goddard had been writing and experimenting since 1919 on vehicles for travel in airless space. There had been much discussion of its possibilities in the daily press during 1930 and 1931. Personally I did not quite understand what it was all about, but I recollected one evening seeing posted on the notice board in the Museum of Natural History word to the affect that the American Interplanetary Society was holding a meeting. I had been slightly amazed when I had made inquiries and learned that his society had for its object the furtherance of plans for travel to other planets. But all this was insufficient to prepare me for Haworth's photograph.

Mason's clear-cut features were in profile as I turned to him. His eyes flashed eagerly and his jaw tensely clenched.

"You actually flew out that distance and returned safely?"

"My dear Mason," Haworth answered amusedly, "I did so four times."

"Why be surprised?" he continued. "Esnault-Pelterie and Herman Oberth have both published detailed scientific discussions of such a possibility. Goddard in this country has built and flown successful rocket vehicles—not to any great height, perhaps, but distance is a mere matter of proportion. I have just gone a little further along the road of discovery."

"But," I interposed, "are we then to understand that our proposed scientific expedition is to take us into space in this—this rocket, is it not? And our goal is to be...?"

But Mason was on his feet and starting for the door of the restaurant.

"Come along," he called. "Hurry before this dream ends and we all wake up!"

And we left that place with the stares of the other diners following us.

Haworth had a car and chauffeur outside the Grandison, waiting. This visible sign of wealth gave me a sense of the reality of things. We headed for Connecticut, voluble and excited. But I had one major puzzle still to be solved.

"This car," I commenced doubtfully, "proceeds along the road because the wheels push it forward with great force. An airplane travels rapidly and powerfully through the atmosphere because the propeller has air to grip on. But how, may I ask, can any vehicle travel forward under power if there is nothing but empty space about it? On what will the engines expend their thrust?"

Mason shook his head. "You stick to your photographs and be a good little naturalist, Bigelow. You don't understand physics."

"But I must understand this!"

"Very well, the principle of recoil is what propels a rocket. For every action there must be an equal and opposite action. Are you satisfied?"

"I don't know quite what you are talking about. Suppose I am in space. I want to move to the left. How shall I proceed to do so?"

Haworth interrupted, "Suppose there are two barrels in space, fastened end to end. You, Bigelow, are in one of the barrels. In the other is merely some ballast of stones. Between the two barrels is a small charge of dynamite."

I NODDED understandingly.

"Now my problem is to move you to the left, eh?"

I began to see light.

"The dynamite explodes. The two barrels are thrown violently apart. The ballast is thrown away to the right but the barrel that contains Mr. Stephen Bigelow is moved to the left. *Quod erat demonstrandum!*"

"That's so!" I cried. "But such an explosion would hardly be called power flight. How would you proceed after that?"

"Very simply. Instead of one barrel to throwaway, I will have ten thousand. One after the other I hurl them from me, each one lending the force of its recoil to my vessel, which attains huge speeds.

"Naturally enough, I do not use real barrels—they are purely figurative. In practice the most efficient thing to throwaway is the waste gaseous product of an explosion or of steady combustion. From the tail of my vessel the white-hot gases pour at a speed of more than two miles a second! Is it any wonder that after a few seconds of this discharge the ship moves rapidly back in recoil from this roaring exhaust?"

"But can that produce power enough?"

"Wait until you have been deafened and thrilled by its fury!"

I had begun, at last, to understand the matter when we turned down the lane of our adventure the week before. But this time we had the main gate opened wide for us. The red-faced keeper was eyeing us phlegmatically. Haworth called him over to the side of the car.

"Jones! This is Mr. Mason and this is Mr. Bigelow. They are going to be with me for some weeks. They will help me run the *Asteroid.*"

It was a small triumph, but Jones was as impassive as ever. Mason leaned past me and handed him a dollar.

"I think both Mr. Bigelow and myself should start even!" he remarked.

I caught a twinkle of amusement in Haworth's eye and we drove on. The road came suddenly around a sharp turn and we rolled to a stop before a fine Colonial mansion.

Mason and I were intent upon an instant visit to the ship. A walk of a hundred yards through a strip of woods brought us to the shore of the lake, beside a most unusual building. We had seen this before from a distance. It was huge and in shape suggested an old-fashioned grain elevator, painted black. A small door gave us access to the interior and we pressed eagerly inside, Haworth following us. Now for the first time we realized the enormous proportions of the vessel we had seen. Soft and sheer she gleamed above our heads a full hundred feet or more, until her tapering nose was lost in the dusk of the hangar.

Haworth patted the metal hull affectionately. "Tried and tested," he said, "and a sweet job, by and large!" He stepped outside a moment and called for "Bill." Bill proved to be a capable-looking mechanic who came up to the door of the great shed chewing a straw and eyeing Mason and myself curiously. We were introduced.

"She's all finished, Mr. Haworth," he said, "except for fitting her into the first step. I have the new liquefying plant running now, filling the main oxygen tanks over in the cove."

Haworth turned to us. "Of course this ship here isn't nearly large enough for an extended trip at really high speeds. This is just the paying cargo, so to speak, that will fit into the nose of the actual vessel. That will be more than eight times as large. We'll see her later on. She's completely finished and being fueled now—half a mile down the lake.

"The big ship—the 'first step' we call her—starts off into space and takes us out until her fuel is gone. Then we discard her and go the rest of the way in the *Asteroid* here. And even the *Asteroid* is only a second step. She carries a little eighty-ton vessel in her nose that will make the final stages of the return flight with us inside."

"How big is the first step, then?"

"About five thousand tons," replied Haworth, and Bill nodded confirmation.

"What fuel do you use?"

"Gasoline and liquid oxygen. You see, Bigelow, there isn't any air where we are going, so we have to take along oxygen in order to burn the fuel. And the fuel isn't exactly gasoline—there are one or two things added that make a deal of difference in results. You know how much more efficient ethyl gas is than ordinary gasoline? Well, ethyl gas isn't the end of the story by any means. We've got a fuel several times better for our purpose than pure gasoline. I'll show you the formula later on, but that is one of the things not to be made public.

"Each step is a complete ship. It has fuel tanks and pumps and a refrigerating system and an explosion chamber for burning the fuel. It has exhaust tubes and steering tubes for propelling the ship. But, of course, only the final eighty-ton vessel has a cabin or a control system. My experimental and test flights have all been made in the *Asteroid*—the second step with the little vessel in its nose. She weighs 640 tons, 80 of which are the cargo. This cargo consists of the little vessel in which is placed myself and all equipment. It costs only about $40,000 to fuel the *Asteroid*—a two-step unit—so I have used her on all test flights to save expense."

"To save expense!"

"Yes. To fuel the entire three-step unit would cost over $300,000," explained Haworth. "Moreover, there's, no need to test the whole. If two steps work properly, then so will three. As a matter of fact, I'm all through testing. We're about ready now for the actual voyage."

"Where?" shot Mason, his eyes bright with excitement.

Haworth looked at him a moment in silent approval. "Good man! That's a question you must help me decide." He consulted his watch. "It's five now. I suggest we go up to the house and have some food and spend the entire evening determining that very point. It might make some difference in construction and equipment."

CHAPTER THREE
Final Preparations

BUT I was unwilling to depart from the vicinity of the hangar until I had been inside the *Asteroid*. Haworth led the way up a ladder of aluminum streamlined rungs let into the hull. One by one we labored up the vertical ascent and crowded into a tiny vestibule at the top. Haworth used a key and we tumbled through a massive steel doorway into a most peculiar room. Lights were set flush with the walls in all directions. The floor was a circle some fifty feet across. The ceiling was only eight feet high, except at the sides where it extended upward for full thirty feet more. It was as though a huge metal cylinder occupied all the central part of what would otherwise have been a circular room more than thirty feet high and fifty across. In the floor, under this huge cylinder, was a hole some five feet across. Peering through this I observed another room similarly designed, but having its central space occupied by much complicated machinery and tubing.

"That is our sleeping cabin," said Haworth. "This up here is the navigation room."

"And all this?" asked Mason, pointing at the cylinder overhead.

"That is our combined pump and refrigerating plant, for liquid oxygen can only be kept under intensely low temperatures. It is placed in this cabin for the sake of availability. But the center of the room is valueless, anyway. You see, when we are under way with full speed up and the engines silent, we become a free-falling body. There is no gravity. Incidentally, it is the most sickening sensation in the world or out of it. I know, for I have felt it.

"So I designed this ship to revolve as it travels—like a rifle bullet. The rotation causes everything to fall toward the outside-centrifugal force, you know. The faster the ship revolves, the greater is the pressure that acts as an effective substitute for gravity. But, as you can figure for yourselves, that would make these walls seem to be floors. You will find yourself in a sort of gigantic revolving squirrel cage. You can walk around it in a hundred steps and be back where you started. If you were here, Bigelow, and Mason upside down on the far wall there, you would each seem to look 'up' and see the other standing head down from the 'ceiling'!"

Mason called from the hole in the floor, through which he was peering on hands and knees: "And so this is where we sleep?"

Haworth lay down beside him. Four cots were suspended from pivoting supports, so as to always hang in a horizontal position. Interesting-looking apparatus and cabinets and lockers could be seen here and there on the walls and set into the floor.

"Food and rest department," explained Haworth. "Everything has been boiled down to the lightest possible weight, but without undue skimping. I flatter myself that there is provision for every comfort aboard. All of it is in that room."

"Books?" I asked.

"I've solved that problem with the Encyclopedia Britannica. It's out of sight behind that water tank."

"Drinks?" suggested Mason.

"Of course," said Haworth. "Beer and wine take up too much room, but there are whiskey, brandy and rum. For food we have a large refrigerator and can feast on fresh meat and eggs the whole trip. But plenty of canned food is packed away, just in case it is needed."

The mention of food reminded us that we were hungry and we made our way back to the vestibule. Haworth made us wait while he shut the metal door behind us.

"Test conditions," he explained. "Ever since she was finished I have kept artificial atmosphere going in her. In actual operation the outer door of this air lock entrance would be closed as well."

"You mean that inside there we were breathing artificial air?"

"Certainly. Why do you ask?"

"Because it was fresh and pure. How long has the cabin been hermetically sealed?"

"More than twelve months. Oh, it is thoroughly tested. We shall not perish from lack of atmosphere. I promise you."

We climbed down the metal rungs. In the gloom of the hangar the vessel rose enormous—suggestive. I realized more and more what was portending and my enthusiasm mounted with every step back to Haworth's house.

After dinner we sat in a huge library and smoked and drank pre-prohibition nectar. "If we were to go to the moon," said Haworth, "we would have to wear diving-suits to walk around on the ground—because there's no atmosphere on the moon."

"Even on Mars," said Mason, "there's so little air that we would have to wear an oxygen helmet."

"Now on Venus…"

"But seriously," I put in, "there's more than a quarter million miles of space between us and the moon, Mars or Venus are several hundred times as far. Why not at least start with the moon? Surely that is enough of a trip! Later on, perhaps…"

But Haworth interrupted. "Distance makes little difference. Only the additional time involved in accomplishing it. To reach the moon, the *Asteroid* would have to travel about seven miles a second as it left our atmosphere. She would pick up that speed in the first ten minutes of travel. After that we would shut off the engines and coast along to our destination—whatever it might be. The moon would require a few days coasting—Mars would take a few months."

"Coast along for a few months!"

"Why of course!" put in Mason. "There is no air to resist the motion. Gravity grows steadily slighter and seven miles a second is just fast enough so that the pull of gravity would never stop our vessel entirely. On she would go through space, her progress getting slower and slower, but never ceasing."

I was by now nodding my agreement. Of course! The Earth itself, was she not just coasting along around the sun? She had been doing so for millions of years, making a steady eighteen miles a second. I simply had not thought of it that way.

"Now Venus," Mason was saying, "is the one planet nearest the Earth both in position and in size. It has a very dense atmosphere indeed. Its surface is completely hidden behind the clouds, which would temper the great heat of the sun, for the planet is closer to the sun than is the Earth. In all the heavens, this is the one planet, so far as we know, where it is at least possible for man to live a natural life— untrammeled by pressure suits and cumbrous aids to breathing. The moon is a barren waste. Mars—just possibly Mars might be barely habitable by a race of super-mountaineers, used to the thin air. But Venus is where we should first point our flight!"

"But," said Haworth, "there are other factors besides atmosphere. Take temperature, for instance. Some astronomers say that Venus keeps one face always toward the sun and the other always toward outer space, if that were so, then the former would be boiling hot and the latter very cold."

MASON nodded, as one who meets an expected obstacle. "The latest tests show definitely that the dark side of Venus radiates heat. Now if this dark side never turned itself to the rays of the sun it could not be in the least warm, for even a dense atmosphere could not prevent it cooling in the course of ages. Besides, if we believe the atmosphere will prove too warm, we can always land near the North or South Poles of Venus and proceed from there toward the equator until, or unless, the temperature becomes unbearable."

A great deal more was said on both sides. But we ended our evening's discussion with a toast to our determined goal.

"To Venus!"

What was more important to my peace of mind, Haworth came out frankly and simply. Omitting nothing, he told us his entire story of the conception and building of the *Asteroid*. To my mind, he presented himself as a sane and sober worker, thoroughly grounded in his subject. My own knowledge of engineering was quite insufficient to determine the practicability of our enterprise. I was forced to rely on Haworth's integrity. But by the end of that evening I had quite determined to trust my life to his obvious skill and knowledge.

This is hardly the time or place for a resume of his life. Only his extreme reticence about his affairs in public persuades me to mention the highlights in very brief fashion.

Bereft suddenly of his parents and embarrassed with unwanted millions, he had retired to his Connecticut estate and nursed his grief in solitude. He determined to continue his studies and had a superb laboratory built for his experiments.

Month after month he worked methodically and patiently, making minor discoveries in several fields of knowledge. Then he evolved a theory for control of liquid fuels in rocket spaceships—a subject that had, it appeared, always fascinated him. He applied his entire faculties to the problem and spared neither effort nor expense. No less than twelve very expensive models had been built and rejected, one after the other before the design for the *Asteroid* was tried.

He had endeavored to maintain as much secrecy as possible—not only from policy, but for fear of ridicule, to which he had thoughtlessly exposed himself once or twice. To this end, such workmen and technical assistants as he had needed had been carefully selected and employed to reside permanently on the estate, which was well guarded, as we had discovered on our first brief visit.

With the completion of the *Asteroid* herself, test flights (chiefly by night) had been made at low speeds, comparatively speaking. Haworth had used the lake both for starting and landing his ship, which, indeed, could not land its great tonnage safely on any other medium than water. He told us of his first trip without emotion, describing his sensations in cold medical terms and couching his language with so much quiet reserve that the enthusiasm he might justly have expressed, lodged itself in his hearers. Here was a man, I felt, whom I could trust to proceed with sanity and caution. Mason, I could sense, shared my feelings.

Whether it was the wine we drank, or the heady nature of our discussion and plans, I do not know, but I lay for hours on Haworth's guest bed, clad in his pajamas laid out for me by his valet, unable to sleep. My head was in a whirl of excitement.

I could not help wondering, as I lay reflecting upon the happenings of the day, just why three normal human beings should be so glad of an opportunity to leave their native planet. There was no slightest question but that we were glad. I mused upon this lure of the undiscovered. What was this motive of sheer curiosity that drove men to all sorts of unexplainable actions? We had perhaps inherited it from our Simian ancestors, for it was as natural as breathing.

Why had Columbus voyaged to the Americas? Was it purely an attempt to reach the Indies, or had the divine urge driven him on? Why was Marco Polo not content with his native Venice? Why were Englishmen, though professing an overpowering love for their little island, such inveterate wanderers?

On the one hand, I reflected, a thrilling plunge into the abyss, perhaps to end in oblivion, unknown to the world—or perhaps to result in fame and glory for us all, with the fine thrill of achievement thrown in. But on the other hand, the comforts and convenience of our present life. Soft beds! An instant satisfaction of our whims through the mechanism of modern civilization! An assurance of safety! Today as I write this I cannot see but that the latter picture was the alluring one. But on that night it seemed to me the very antithesis of everything worthwhile. Drab and dull days and nights; old age slowly creeping upon me; desire and zest burning out, year by year, until the dried-up shell of the man loves life no longer. The prospect seemed quite insupportable. Change and adventure had been thrown in my path by fortunate chance. Now it was here, it seemed absolutely essential to existence.

What might be the results of our expedition, supposing it to be successful? The effect would be enormous. As Europe in the earthly sixteenth century awakened from a long sleep, and brave deeds and high adventure strutted the stage of life—so upon our return would the whole, world wake to new possibilities and still wider vistas. But foremost of all was the thought that I, Stephen Bigelow, was to be the naturalist on an expedition to Venus. The first studies ever made of life as it might be found on another planet! Of all the paradises that I could imagine, what could be more enticing?

Fame, success and (above all) interesting, vital, absorbing work! The risks—*pshaw!* For such a reward what were risks? After all, a trip to the Gobi desert or to the jungles of Africa was not without its risks. Everything worth doing entailed a hazard of some sort. I fell asleep and dreamed that I was being greeted at New York upon my return. Thousands of policemen on motorcycles escorted me up Broadway and the people all cheered and threw confetti.

The next morning was Sunday and after breakfast Mason asked for three things: an astronomical almanac, some writing materials, and a little privacy. Haworth had some business to attend to and I wandered by myself down to the lake. I followed the shore and rounding a wooded headland, came upon a scene of exceeding activity. A dozen men stood about a huge silver vessel some three hundred feet in length and more than a hundred feet in diameter. It lay in a cradle of wooden spars and frames. Behind it was a low building of brick with smoke issuing from a tall chimney. There was no noise except for a rhythmic thump and clang that issued from the building and an occasional voice calling for "Bill."

I walked around the vessel and perceived in one end, a huge circular opening, evidently intended to house the *Asteroid*. The other extremity flared out in smooth flanges, which were the exhaust tubes. I peered up one of these. It was about a foot in diameter. I could see only a short distance into the dark interior of the vessel.

BILL came to my side. "Isn't she a pretty job?" he asked. "We're filling her tanks with gas and liquid oxygen now. Inside her the refrigerating pumps are working away to keep the oxygen liquid, but you can't hear them out here. I'm going to test the ignition. Want to see it?"

I did of course. Bill called to the men and everyone left the vicinity of the exhaust end of the ship. Bill took me into the brick building and walked up to a series of dials and levers against one wall.

"We have everything connected up in the workshop here. When the *Asteroid* is fitted in her, the controls will be in the navigating cabin, naturally enough. Now I'm going to give her just enough fuel to stir her slightly."

I looked out the doorway at the ship. The exhaust tubes, I noticed, all faced the lake. Suddenly a deafening roar broke out like thunder. A fierce blast of flame licked out far over the lake and then vanished. The huge hull moved a few inches in her wooden cradle and was still again.

"Everything fine," remarked Bill in the startling silence. "But I'll have to scrape the spark points in the lower port sector. It seemed to me they lagged just a little bit."

I left them at it and walked back toward the hangar, feeling more than a little thoughtful. Haworth was in the shed when I arrived. It was lunchtime, he announced, and we proceeded back to the house.

Mason was looking for us. "If we want to start this year," he said, "we had better get busy. As nearly as I can see we should plan to leave about May 26th to get the full benefit of the position of Venus in her orbit."

"But," I objected, "that leaves us only four weeks."

"Fine!" approved Haworth. "We won't have to wait so long."

Mason and I left after lunch. Haworth sent his car in with us. We reached our apartment and devoted the rest of the day and evening to our personal preparations. For myself, these consisted largely in a list of people to see and things to do in the next few days. Cameras and film, compact folding specimen boxes, a few indispensable books and instruments—all of which I already possessed. The following day I had to make arrangements about leaving the paper in charge of my quite capable assistant, Jackson. Beyond that, I reflected, there was really nothing absolutely essential.

I shall omit the ordinary detail of the next few days. On Wednesday night we packed the last of our things and left the apartment for the last time. Mason told me that he had seen his department head that Monday.

"Friedland took it all right. The term is practically through, anyway, and I've been hinting all winter that I might take next year sabbatical. But he wanted to know where I was going…"

I nodded. The owner of my paper had been curious, as well. I had been forced to tell him outright that my destination was a secret.

"But, Mason, I did tell him this much—that on my return I hoped to have some photographs that would increase the circulation of *Lens and Bellows* more in a week than it had grown during the last ten years! What did you tell Friedland?"

"I said that traveling at thirty miles an hour it would take more than one hundred years for me to arrive; but that, if I lived, I would go there and back in less than a year!"

I laughed. "And he?"

"Threw up his hands and told me to be off!"

We went out to Connecticut that evening so as to be ready the next morning to commence preparations in earnest. Mason was already at breakfast when I went down stairs after a good sleep. He hurried his meal and rushed off to the library. There was, he said, an enormous amount of calculating to be done before we would know where to aim for and when.

"If we can be ready by the 26th of May I can save a great deal of calculating, for it happens that Bisset and Schwartz took that particular date in their book for figuring the relative positions of Venus and Earth. It will save me several solid days of work, and I will need the saving."

As a matter of fact, we saw little or nothing of him from that time on. He had ordered three calculating machines and Haworth had hired him a small staff of assistants. The library hummed with activity. They even went to the length of having their noon meal brought in to them there.

I went over my equipment with Haworth and asked about weapons. He had thought of them already. He showed me the arsenal. He had decided on 32 repeating rifles firing both explosive and solid shells.

"These, plus one portable machine gun (a Lewis) for emergencies, ought to take care of us."

Then there were hatchets, knives, Colt automatics and even a store of tear-gas bombs. He glanced over my cameras and told me I would find better ones already on board. In fact, I could suggest nothing that he had not already thought of and provided for. I finally did add to the equipment certain items of specimen cases, jars of formaldehyde and a powerful and compact microscope. Haworth weighed this in his hand reflectively, but handed it back without comment.

Armed with a detailed plan of the control cabin, I prowled about in the nose of the *Asteroid* marveling at the completeness and quality of her fittings. I spent several days familiarizing myself with everything.

Then Haworth decided the *Asteroid* was several hundred pounds overweight and we spent a hectic two days cutting down on the equipment. My microscope went into the discard with other things. Chiefly these were spare space suits. He left just one suit for each of us. They were much like diving suits, having a metal helmet and heavy rubber body designed to be pumped full of air at fifteen pounds per square inch, pressure. They would be essential should we have to leave the ship when she was not in suitable atmosphere—either on earth or on Venus. And when on Venus they might be needed, for, while there is a dense atmosphere, yet it might prove poisonous.

The last week, the oxygen fuel pumps were put in operation to replenish the *Asteroid's* tanks. A small mountain of gas cylinders was brought in trucks for this purpose and piled outside the shed. Then the water tank had to be filled with fresh water and the air conditioning apparatus tested and refilled with new chemicals. The third step, down the shore of the lake, had been completely fueled by now and its pumps seemed to be keeping the oxygen liquid without too much loss. The next problem was to launch it and fit the *Asteroid* in the hole designed to accommodate her—ready for the final flight.

But, as Haworth pointed out, if we wanted to make a final test flight of the *Asteroid,* we would have to do it before she was fitted to the third step. Mason, when routed out from his figuring, said he didn't care about a test—he would trust all that to Haworth. But Haworth insisted.

"Suppose something happened to me, old man," he argued. "You must know every control on the ship—you particularly, for Bigelow here is not mechanically-minded."

Mason gave in at that. Another twenty-four hours, he said, and his figures would be finished. That would still give us two days before the staring hour. He plunged back into the clatter and count of his computators.

CHAPTER FOUR
"On to Venus"

THE test was on May 24th—a clear day. As we walked over to the hangar I drew in deep lungs-full of air and threw my head back. It was one of those days when a few clouds drift like cotton wool in a smiling sky. But the sky had a new meaning for me now and the clouds were intimate things we should soon meet and pass. Haworth climbed at once up the ladder and out of sight, but Mason and myself walked around the *Asteroid* in the gloom of the shed and I saw Mason put out his hand and pat the cool metal hull as if to reassure himself. Then we went up, Mason first, and into the air lock.

Haworth was below in the living cabin. He called up to us, "Hurry along, you chaps! We start right away."

"But how can we start from the shed here?" I asked, peering over the edge of the hole at him.

"Top swings back. Bill's tending to that now. Come on down—but seal up that air lock first."

Mason shut the vestibule door and turned the long handle that sealed it hermetically. We climbed down and got into the swinging cots with some difficulty, aided near the end of our climb by Haworth's pointing out that there were rungs on the water tank.

"Just a moment, Haworth," Mason said. "It's easy enough to get up in the air, but how do you land the thing?"

"We have wings. This lever here projects short stubby wings out of the side of the *Asteroid*. Didn't I show them to you? We use the wings just as an airplane does, though we have to land pretty fast, of course. But the lake's big enough.

I always come down facing southeast. In case anything went wrong I could always turn on the power again and shoot over to Long Island Sound. But I haven't had to startle the natives there yet and I hope I won't have to this time."

The water tank extended along beside the three cots and on it were set three simple levers—duplicate controls—and a series of dials were visible on the hull wall to indicate altitude, direction and speed. The ship was navigable, of course, without any reference to outside observation. Indeed it would have been difficult to design a window with sufficient structural strength. I will later describe, among other apparatus, our periscope-telescope, which enabled us to take observations en route.

But we were by now strapped in our cots and Haworth's hand was on the starting lever. He looked inquiringly at us.

"There's no shock, you know. The pressure isn't very great, except at full acceleration. These cots are mainly provided in case of an upset—and for sleeping in, naturally. All set? Here goes!"

He pulled the lever and for a second nothing appeared to happen. I had a panicky feeling that the whole thing was a hoax. In that second I realized how much I actually desired to make the trip. Then the ship quivered and swayed very slightly. I was pushed down in my cot the way one is sometimes jerked back into an automobile seat when the driver suddenly steps on the gas. Only I stayed pushed down. I waited breathlessly.

Haworth's voice startled me:

"Look at the altitude dial!"

I blinked disbelievingly, for it read 2000 feet and the hand was sweeping up faster and faster as I stared. It was shaped like a clock—one hand set for feet and one for miles. Now we were two miles up! Now ten—twenty—a hundred! The air-speed indicator stood at one mile a second!

"I'm going to shut off the power," announced our pilot. "Just to show you what it feels like, I won't start the rotator for a few seconds. Hold tight now!"

The speed was almost two miles a second and the height something over two hundred miles when he pushed back the lever. Then and there I lost my breakfast. I have been down a fast toboggan slide and know what it means to "leave your stomach in the air." This was many times worse. My ears buzzed and my head swam. There was a sickening sensation of falling and I clutched my cot as hard as I could, trying to recover the sense of pressure. Presently I felt better. Not altogether right, but better. I felt light-headed and blown-up like a balloon. Haworth was apologizing profusely.

"I didn't dream it would take you that way. It just made me dizzy, not sick at all. How are you, Mason?"

"All right now," replied my friend, "but don't do that again if you value your cuticle!"

And then I noticed that the water tank was above me—not beside me. The hull wall, with its instruments, had somehow turned into a floor. What was happening?

"Your weight is now due to centrifugal force instead of gravity," said Haworth, who saw my puzzled glance.

Mason had figured beforehand that at our speed we would have five minutes to ourselves before the ship lost its headway and would require our attention for a return to earth. I unstrapped myself and stood shakily on my feet.

Mason also looked about him and suddenly gave a great bound into the air. He struck his back against the tank overhead. While he swore loudly, I warily essayed a few steps and found myself light as a feather. I have since estimated our weight at about six earthly pounds each. On the real trip, later on, we increased this by making a faster rotation of the ship. Of course, the faster the ship spun, the greater the centrifugal force and the greater our sense of weight. So exactly, in fact, does this force imitate the observable phenomena of gravity, that it might suggest to an inquiring mind a possible clue for the solution of that enigma of nature. Is gravity really akin to magnetism after all?

We walked through into what was now the adjoining room. Haworth, who had preceded us, was staring into the periscope glass and turning knobs eagerly.

"We must be pointing away from the earth," he said. "I can't locate her anywhere." He set in motion the ship's gyroscope and I noticed the direction pointer swing around until it pointed straight toward the nose of the ship.

"Here she is!" cried Mason, who had joined him. I came up and looked down at the glass where I saw a great rounded section of my native land. Clouds obscured much of Virginia, but I could make out Cape Cod with great detail, standing out into a Lilliputian ocean.

Our landing maneuvers now occupied our immediate attention. The speed we had acquired was less than two miles a second and to attain this we had partially exhausted the fuel contents of only one step of our ship. It had not been necessary to jettison any of the structure, as it would have been had a still higher speed been required.*

HAWORTH now projected our wings and Mason maneuvered the periscope to keep our objective in view. Gradually the picture below grew larger and finally instead of being rounded, the landscape flattened out and the edges seemed to curl up. Details appeared in the scene beneath us

---

*I might mention that from each step protrudes a rudimentary fin from which can be pushed out short wings, one set of wings for each of the three steps in the complete ship. The projecting power is furnished by the pumps and a small wheel in the control room regulates the whole system.

and suddenly began to move sideways.

"We're flattening out," said our leader quietly. "I want you to watch the altimeter closely, Bigelow. You, Mason, get located on that periscope and keep it pointed right!"

I was somehow not alarmed in the least. I stood leaning against the water tank. Haworth had to turn on the power for a moment once or twice and used the directional rockets half a dozen times. That was all. I watched the altitude indicator creep down again to a mile; to a thousand feet. Then I glanced at the periscope glass. There were the familiar Connecticut hills sweeping by at a great rate. I glanced at the air-speed indicator, which now showed two hundred miles an hour.

"Hold tight!" called Haworth and in the glass I saw suddenly at close range a gleam of water. There was a blue and white splash and my knees gave way beneath me as the ship lurched, rolled a few seconds and started turning. Then they gave way completely, for the floor turned up sideways and became the sidewall of our chamber once again. I fell heavily against the partition, now beneath me. My companions had held on and, as I scrambled to my feet, they asked anxiously if I had been hurt. Fortunately, I had not.

There was a collapsible canvas boat in the ship's supplies and we lowered this to the water's surface and Mason climbed down and got it opened out and afloat on the water. Then we all got in and he rowed us to shore.

Bill and his crew met us. "Quick trip, Mr. Haworth," he said. And I could not believe my eyes when my watch showed ten o'clock! We had been gone altogether twenty-five minutes.

That morning we rested up at the house, but in the afternoon Mason announced that our starting hour was 4:30 on the 26th and he was going to check all the figures he had time for and as often as he could. Whereupon he vanished into the library once more.

Haworth and I went down to supervise the assembly of the *Asteroid* into the first step. By the time we got there it was nearly finished. The huge step had been launched into the waters of the lake and floated low and heavy. As we watched, she settled lower still, and finally disappeared beneath the surface.

"Good Lord! What is the matter?"

"Wait and see."

They were towing up the *Asteroid*. Men were working over the sunken hull and I now observed several large hose lines led from the depths up to an attending scow on which was some pumping machinery. The *Asteroid* was carefully placed just over the spot where the first step had sunk and men with air-lines extending over the water to the shore rowed about, fastening them here and there.

When all was in place, Bill stood on the scow and waved his arm twice. Slowly the *Asteroid* settled. Just before she, in turn, disappeared, she halted and began to rise slowly.

Haworth and I had taken a small boat and rowed out to the scene of activities. The work was stopped while he made an inspection. Finally he approved of everything and the air was once more forced into containers in the step below the water. I now perceived the intent of the operations and admired it hugely. In half an hour the step had risen above the surface. Half-swallowed in her bow cavity was the *Asteroid*. The complete three-step space ship floated on the water, ready for the final fueling.

Haworth had calculated it would be easier to fuel the vessel on the lake, rather than tow her to shore again. The first step and the third step were already fully loaded with gas and liquid oxygen and there remained only the second step, which we had nearly exhausted of fuel in making our test trip.

We departed, leaving this final work in charge of the men. Half a dozen scows loaded with oxygen cylinders and an emergency liquefying refrigerator were busily at work by the time we had rowed to shore and turned to give the vessel a departing glance.

This work continued on the 25th. That day seemed made up of a thousand hours, each hour some years in length! Haworth was busy with a man who had come out from the city. Making his will, I presumed, though he never told me. I could not tear myself away from the vessel and sat by the hour watching Bill make the final arrangements. The men were all leaving that morning, he said.

"Mr. Haworth thinks it just as well to have no witnesses, I guess."

"But don't they know where we are going?"

"No," said Bill, "and probably wouldn't care if they did."

"But you will see us off?"

Bill flushed slightly. He nodded in silence. Finally he spoke.

"I'm married."

He stared unseeingly across the lake.

"If I weren't…but I am, and that's that!"

I could not help reflecting that Haworth carried the secrecy of the thing to almost unnecessary lengths. Was he planning to tell no one of our expedition until our return?

Evening came at last and the three of us dined soberly enough and smoked in sober meditation for a few hours before turning in.

"Are you both sure you have no friends or relatives you wish notified in case we…don't return?"

"I have an aunt," said Mason. "But I don't know her address."

Haworth laughed affectedly.

We shook hands as we parted for the night.

I HAD a wretched sleep. I thought of all the things that might have happened to us the day before. We had been too lucky for words—that was all! The least thing wrong, and it would have been all over with us. And suppose we had been landing on Venus—dense fog; no way of telling how close to land we were; no assurance that there was any water to come down on! And on the trip, just suppose we hit one fair-sized meteorite traveling at cosmic speed! I thought of how a bullet made of paper had been shot through a sheet of tin by some experimenter years ago. We would be the sheet of tin!

Only the thought of ridicule stopped me from backing out altogether the next morning. Mason afterwards confessed that it was much the same with him. He had calculated all night our chances of a successful return and, what with a nightmare or two to affect his figures, the answer came out exactly 480,972,635 chances to one! Haworth apparently slept like a log.

I was not in too great a hurry that morning, I fear. Haworth kept trying to make me move faster but I took my time. We were really all ready by three in the afternoon, but I kept "forgetting" things we would be sure to need. The last time I thought of cards and a cribbage board. I'm glad I thought of them, but he said it was the last straw and dragged me down to the boat where Mason was sitting, staring silently at the water. We rowed out to the vessel and Haworth and I climbed up the ladder, leaving Mason to fold up the boat. When we got to the air lock we heard a cry from below and looked down.

Mason had fallen into the lake and was climbing up the rungs dripping water and swearing. So we pulled the boat up as it was and folded it together in the vestibule, while Mason stamped around shedding wet clothes and climbed around down in the living cabin, trying to find dry ones.

It was a few minutes past four when we were all in our cots. Our calculations had been arranged for a start at exactly four-thirty, so we had to wait twenty minutes. I had to fight myself hard every one of the twenty to keep myself from unstrapping my legs and getting down that ladder to solid earth again. It was warm in the cabin, but not warm enough to account for the perspiration that poured over me!

"Ready!" said Haworth warningly.

And then for a certainty I knew I could not stick it out. But as I started to get up on one elbow and had opened my mouth, in fact, to call to Haworth, he pulled the lever. I was forced back against the cot. We had started!

Our course, once calculated, was very simple to follow. Given an exact starting time, all that was necessary at first was to aim straight for a definite portion of the skies. We aimed for the star Kappa in Leo. It was Mason's job to keep the periscope glass focused on this point exactly at the start. Every second of travel he had to veer away from it by fifteen seconds of arc, to allow for the rotation of the earth. All other factors were taken into consideration when fixing the original aiming point. Haworth kept the ship lined up with the periscope direction indicator. I did what Haworth told me from time to time. As all our instruments and controls, even the periscope glass, were duplicated in our living quarters, all this could easily be done from our cots.

For eight minutes we lay there. Every little while Mason would exclaim "There she goes!" and twist frantically at his controls.

"North declination two minutes of arc!" Haworth called out.

Then it would be "East by north a second!" and once it was "four minutes south! Quick! Five! —ah, there she comes!" while Mason swore and twisted away.

Then abruptly Haworth pushed up the power lever and pulled it back again.

"There goes the first step!" he said grimly.

So far the power flight had been made almost in silence. But when the first step was dropped away, the steady pressure we felt became realized in its terrific, powerful force, for the sound of the exhaust suddenly increased to very audible proportions. It filled me with its message of vast, blasting power. When it, in turn, suddenly ceased, I glanced at Haworth in surprise. He was advancing the rotating lever and I scarcely felt the dizziness. Our cots swung around at ninety degrees and the walls became our floor once more.

"That's that!" I said and forced a painful smile.

"You don't have to watch that periscope any longer," said he to Mason. Power's off, you know."

Mason sat up in his cot frowning slightly.

"It doesn't seem right," he objected, "to be hurtling through space at seven miles a second without anyone looking to see where we're going!"

Haworth laughed, his black whiskers framing a jovial cavern. A great load seemed lifted from his mind.

"No power, no steering. We have already steered her! Now we are coasting to a stop. We'll coast for about three months, and there's only one thing we can do about it. Can any bright child tell me what that is?"

But I thought I knew the answer to that, and I was first at the liquor closet. Whiskey straight, and we all needed it!

How calmly they take it, you exclaim. Well, I don't know about Mason and Haworth but, speaking for myself, the above account leaves out a great deal. To be frank, I was so nervous and alarmed during the start that I scarcely felt my discomfort. After a minute or two the steady pressure affected my thoughts to the complete exclusion of other feeling. I found it difficult to draw breath, due, I suppose, to the increased weight of my body, which during power flight was some four times as heavy as its normal one hundred and eighty pounds. My eyelids were almost too heavy to support themselves and I noticed that Mason and Haworth were both peering at their instruments through half-closed lids.

While the throb and sound of power held the ship there was nothing absolutely terrifying or strange about it all. That sensation came when the rocket motors were shut off. The stillness was like a blow. I stood beside my cot and contemplated the dials before me. The altitudinometer was no longer working, for we had left the atmosphere of the earth! Its dial had marked only as high as 250 miles and there it remained, although I knew we must be thousands of miles away from our native land by this time.

The speedometer (indicating the speed of air past our hull) had of course dropped to zero, for there was no longer any air to rush past us. Mason and Haworth had gone into the pump room and were busy checking our course with Mason's careful figures. I was alone in the cabin. A sudden panic came upon me as I realized our position. We were lost in absolute space. I realized that now there could be no turning back. Our departure was final. We must go on to Venus—a strange and perhaps terrible adventure.

CHAPTER FIVE
Tense Moments

THEN the whine of the ventilator fan broke the silence. One of my companions must have turned it on to set the atmospheric conditioner in operation. This droning monotony remained with us for the next three months. It frequently affected our nerves, yet we all agreed that it was preferable to the absolute silence that otherwise would have pervaded our vessel.

It changed my train of thought entirely (possibly the stimulant I had just taken helped) and I realized once more the thrill of adventure. I had not felt this so strongly since Haworth's first announcement of the purpose of his expedition. I remember saying to myself, "Why, you stupid oaf, you're going to Venus!" And a new exhilaration came upon me and carried me into the next room to join my companions. I wanted all of a sudden to see where we were—to look out on the illimitable space in which we traveled—to gaze longingly at our shining goal and look back exultantly at the work-a-day world we had left!

I rushed over to the glass to peer into the periscope. It magnified some twenty diameters and happened to be pointed into a starry region that included a small section of the Milky Way. Never with earthly language can I describe what it looked like. The stars were smaller than we see them from the Earth, for they were not magnified by two hundred miles of atmosphere. But their brightness was increased a thousand-fold. Like jewels on black velvet they lay, each one a pinpoint of blinding brilliance. And so thick and deep did they carpet the cosmos as to draw a gasp of delight from me.

I knew how to turn the ship and periscope from watching Haworth on the test flight and I spent a solid hour then and there bringing sight after sight into view. One of the first things I looked for was in Orion—the dark "horsehead" nebula near Zeta of that constellation. But I found it appeared not very different from photographs I had seen on earth. My vision was clearer, of course, and I could see without any doubt that the dark spot was no "hole in space" but a real, opaque object from behind which light of distant stars streamed revealingly. I called Mason over to watch it with me and he did so, withdrawing from the instrument at last with visible emotion.

But the sight of the receding Earth was of the greatest beauty and interest to me. It was as if my heartstrings were attached to it and almost seemed to snap with the strain of separation. Tears came to my eyes. The globe was almost fully illuminated by the sun and both North and South America lay in full view. In fact not all the surface could be seen in the field of the instrument at once—although this was quite possible a day or two later.

"Well," said Haworth, munching a biscuit and sipping a glass of whiskey soda. "They will be just about getting the news at the Associated Press offices by now."

At this surprising announcement both Mason and myself turned to stare at our leader.

He had the grace to blush.

"No use keeping the secret once we've started," he added in explanation. "Let 'em laugh if they can now! We're in space!"

"What did you do?"

"Sent the Associated Press a dozen pictures of the *Asteroid* with a brief scientific description and a signed statement of the purpose of our voyage."

"Good Lord!"

"But then, down there...!"

I turned again to the glass, as if at that distance I could detect the streets of New York as the newspapers poured out wet from the presses with headlines four inches high. I tried to visualize Chicago's Loop with office workers pouring out that evening to greet the astounding news. But in the glass the Great Lakes were dark blobs on a misty globe and Chicago with its millions an infinitely microscopic phenomenon.

Mason was frowning thoughtfully. "They'll call us madmen, of course."

Then he smiled. "And so we are!"

"When—or if—we get back," said Haworth quietly, "there will be considerable to say on that subject!"

We were wildly excited, all of us—although Haworth did not show it. Mason was like a small boy and full of spirits. I was little better. It was new and strange to have the center of the cabins always "up" and the outside universe in every direction always seem "down," In the pump room at the partition (formerly the floor at the entrance) there was an eight-foot alley clear of overhead obstruction. One could look up full fifty feet to the ship's hull above. Mason liked this spot. He would run violently "up" the floor until he stood on what seemed to me the "ceiling" and looked down at me, grinning.

"I'm an anthropophagus whose head doth grow between his shoulders," he called. "And you're another!"

Then he leaped violently "down" at me and, weighing about six pounds, as I have said, passed the intervening center of gravity and landed laughingly with both arms around my neck, to save himself from falling to the floor.

We even tried a sort of spatial leapfrog. But this did not turn out to be a success. Mason made a wild leap and struck has head hard against the pump tanks, falling "heavily" to the floor. He was unconscious for ten minutes and only the head of a mathematician, as I pointed out, saved him to posterity. That episode occurred, as it happened, in the first hour of free-falling flight. It sobered us considerably. I suggested we give the ship a greater speed of rotation, in order to increase the gravity and, upon Haworth's agreeing, I turned it on until our spring pound-scale registered seven ounces. At that speed the centrifugal force was almost half as strong as gravity is on earth. My head seemed at once clearer and my body began to feel as if it belonged to me after all.

Haworth had done rather well in the eating line. There was an electric stove for cooking and we had a large refrigerator full of hundreds of pounds of fresh meat and vegetables.* We ate broiled steak and onions our first meal—well washed down, you may be sure. And, as Haworth mentioned proudly, "not a sniff of onion in the ship's sacred air!"

I have promised to describe several other pieces of apparatus and perhaps, while I am in a descriptive mood, I might well do so here. First, our periscope. Up in the nose of the ship is a thick glass lens set in a metal ring whose position is changeable at will from the dials on the periscope glass in the cabin below. Through a simple system of angle lenses, the light rays are brought down a tube, magnified, and led by mirrors to the two observation glasses. The range of

---

*He had a clever arrangement for cooking everything inside an airtight mica box. Back of the stove was a square door the exact size of this stove-cover. It was an air lock leading to the outside of the hull and was for the disposal of garbage—solid, liquid or gaseous. As outside, due to our centrifugal force, was always "down," It was simple to operate, although Mason assured us that offal would follow us through space and when we landed we had better carry umbrellas until the vademecum shower had finished!

observation, or rather the angle of vision, is about 45 degrees in any direction from the line in which the vessel's nose is pointing.

During free-falling flight in space, when it is necessary to keep the ship in rotation, the image seems also to rotate in the periscope glass. But a star at that distance is so minute this does not matter for directional observations. And Haworth had arranged for this when he designed the *Asteroid*. The whole system of lenses occupied the exact centerline of the vessel and could be rotated automatically to balance this effect. Occasionally the automatic device did not function in exact time and the image would wobble and blur in the glass, but usually the visibility was satisfactory in the extreme.

When in the atmosphere of the Earth (or of Venus) the wings are protruded and terrestrial gravity is felt. Rotation is then, of course, stopped altogether. And at such times—landing or taking off—when accurate, reliable vision is required, it is present, for the lens-tube is then stationary.

I was puzzled at first to determine how to make observations of the Earth we were leaving. I wanted some photographs. But Haworth, when asked said, "Why not turn the ship's nose back toward the Earth?"

"But we are going to Venus!"

"Well? We don't have to go nose first, do we?"

And he solved the problem very simply by turning the gyroscope control until the receding earth came into view and I got some fine pictures. It is really remarkable how clearly the pictures came out in spite of the many thicknesses of glass intervening between the camera and the object. I attribute this to the crystal-clear space in which we fell—end-first, as it happened!

FALLING! That reminds me of my first sleep on board. It is singular how little sleep one needs in space. This is due, possibly, to the lessened weight. I had four meals before I felt in the least sleepy, (There is no night or day, as you can see for yourself if you think about it). I went to bed and dreamed of falling. Hours and hours I fell. In between these times I wakened and thought of things. I thought of the fallen angel in Milton's poem who fell, twisting and turning in space, for seven days and nights. I could not help thinking how ill I should have been under his circumstances! And then I wondered whether he carried any food or air with him and realized that I must be half-asleep to think of such a silly idea. I dreamed some more and woke again.

I thought of Jack London's story about primitive man's racial fear of falling from trees. I wondered if some future super-human would retain in his race heritage this super-fear of cosmic falling.

We had agreed to stand six-hour watches (although there was no real necessity) and I stood five watches in a row before I dared go to sleep again. But when I did finally climb into my cot once more I slept the sleep of one who has mastered space travel. I slept for twenty, solid, blessed hours.

But to finish my descriptions: Air is supplied from the oxygen fuel tanks as we need it. It is purified by a small air-conditioner in the pump room that sucks it in and spews it out to the tune of a monotonous whine from a wire-caged fan. Heat we have in plenty. One side of the vessel is always exposed to the fierce rays of the sun and we must depend upon pure radiation from the dark side to counteract it. Usually we were uncomfortably warm. Haworth had to keep an auxiliary refrigerator turned on most of the time to get any comfort in the cabins.

Fortunately, all this had been foreseen and, as the total power required to operate refrigerators, electric dynamo for lights and fan and the cooking stove combined was insignificant compared to one second of power flight, there was nothing to worry about. Haworth had figured a fifty percent safety margin in estimating fuel requirements.

Well, I seem to have covered nearly everything. Oh yes! No baths! We had plenty of water later on, due to our fifty percent reserve, and could wash our faces and hands as we liked. But at the start we were conserving all we could, and mighty grimy and filthy we were, too, before we had been a month out. At least Mason and Haworth were—fortunately I couldn't see myself. Haworth particularly, with his crop of jet-black whiskers, looked uncomely. Mason and myself were (at least nominally) shaven.

And now comes the one part of the voyage best glossed over. Three months! I wonder if any of you have spent three months in two rooms? Not even putting our head out of a window, mind! It gets tiresome, I tell you. For the first week or two we were busy enough. Mason in calculating our course all over again, and then in calculating our return based upon a two weeks' stay on Venus. After that he calculated sundry things. The most admired was a computation of our chances of being hit by a meteorite. It came out well into the millions. I may say here in regard to this pet bug-a-boo of critics of space travel that we sighted one meteor during our entire trip. It broke up our cribbage tournament for two hours.

"Come quick!" Haworth called from the periscope. "Something out there towards Vega."

We crowded around the glass and watched a black dot grow rapidly larger. It passed within perhaps ten miles of us, we guessed. And if that guess were accurate, it would have been about two-and-twenty feet through.

I, on my part, spent the first ten days busily with my camera. As official cameraman on the ship, I took the Earth about once an hour, I believe, except while I was sleeping. I photographed Mars, Venus, Saturn and Jupiter and would have got Pluto, the outermost planet, but we couldn't locate it in the glass. Oh yes! Mason figured on that too. Took him two days and I aimed exactly where he pointed but could not see a sign of Pluto. I snapped several films in the general direction, however, and it may turn out on the plates when they can be subjected to careful study.

Then to further lengthen my labors, all the films had to be developed and prints made.

Haworth kept busy climbing about the pumps and machinery. No matter how often he had checked a gadget, he seemed always to enjoy doing it once again, "to make sure."

But after the first two weeks photography palled. We were getting so far away from the Earth that there seemed little use in further pictures of the bright little globe—less than half as large as the moon appears on earth. I had taken all the other subjects I could think of.

Mason had made a final calculation bearing on the probable percentage of error in his other calculations! The three of us gravitated mutually toward the cribbage board.

We started a tournament at ten cents a game. About all I remember of the next two months was the fact that I was seventy-six games ahead of Mason and twenty ahead of Haworth. Haworth, in turn, had thirty-seven games more than Mason. That made me champion and I believe I was prouder of that fact than I should have been.

While two of us were playing, the other one would read the Encyclopedia Britannica and it is amusing to note the things one can find in that mine of information. When anyone came across an interesting statement, he would read it aloud to the others.

"Did you know that the Malay race is distinct from the whites, yellows and blacks?" calls Mason. "I always thought they were almost the same as the Chinese, only brown."

And from the next room came the subdued sounds of Haworth snoring, for it was his rest period. There it is. Life on a rocket ship—a thrilling journey to a new world!

This may not sound like a serious scientific expedition, but it must be remembered that we were absolutely helpless now to change our fate. We had to amuse ourselves or—do worse, perhaps. Men must laugh, whether on the way to the guillotine or to Venus. And when that last day comes when the freezing world circles uselessly a blackening, heatless sun and the last coal has been burned and the atmosphere freezes in a fine snowfall and the last hope is gone—then men will probably have to be amused just the same.

If, indeed, any men remain on Earth by then. Surely everything worth saving in the human race will be far away and safe on a new world, circling a younger sun! Was it for nothing that we made our expedition?

Scientific expeditions are not always amusing. And in that case trouble ensues, sooner or later. Ask any famous explorer whether he objects to a vein of humor in his men! We three were, I suppose, as nearly harmonious in our tastes and prejudices as would be possible to imagine. The importance of this fact cannot be stressed too much as the long, dull, dayless time ticked by.

HAWORTH'S genuinely interesting ideas could set us afire with enthusiasm and Mason's droll manner and absurd wit, time and again, provoked us to abandoned laughter. I recollect one bad moment only.

Mason had made some amusing remark at which I laughed. Haworth, however, merely frowned impatiently. I could see Mason's cheek grow red as he turned away and sat himself down moodily with a volume of the Encyclopedia. This might have developed trouble then and there, but was interrupted violently by Haworth's discovery of the meteor, mentioned previously.

But we all of us seemed to act and talk unnaturally. A definite sense of nervous strain weighed upon us. I remember how irritated I was because Haworth kept poking about in the living cabin—checking and again checking supplies of food in the refrigerator and testing and examining the cooking apparatus.

Mason was still sensitive in his bearing toward Haworth and when the latter called out to him and asked if he would "hand him the food chart." Mason did not seem to hear. After a minute Haworth came into the pump room where we were sitting and got the chart himself.

"Getting deaf?" he remarked rather bitterly.

And Mason rose and turned his chair about so as to face away from him. There he sat in sullen silence.

Haworth had paused at Mason's action. His face grew almost as black as his beard.

"Will you be so decent as to speak when you're spoken to?" he demanded.

Mason was silent.

"Damn you, Mason!" shouted Haworth, reaching out an arm and seizing the other's shoulder. "Who do you think you are?"

Mason leaped to his feet, tearing loose from Haworth's grasp. He whirled, his eyes blazing. I had seen Mason angry once or twice before and at such times he is usually inarticulate and sullen. He was so now, and stood speechless, glaring at Haworth.

I was aghast. But I was determined to let the thing develop no further. I strode between them.

"The man that says another word is going to be sorry," I announced firmly. "For I'll knock him down!"

I was determined to do so, too. I was physically more than a match for either one of them, as they well knew, but whether this affected the course of events or whether common sense came to them both at the same time, I do not know. Haworth strode off into the next room without a word and Mason sat in his chair once more and appeared to have resumed his reading.

I could feel the skin tighten over my cheekbones. I felt badly about the quarrel and more than a little irritated at my companions. I wandered over to the air conditioner dials and studied them unseeingly for fully five minutes, thinking deeply. Then I found myself examining them with casual interest.

The thermometer read 72 degrees Fahrenheit. A sort of barometer recorded absolute air pressure; another dial indicated the moisture content of the air in our cabin, and a fourth showed the electric potential.

I stared at this latter dial in some surprise, for its needle had moved around to the very limit of its ability and, as I recollected, it was supposed to show only a slight elevation above zero. *

Hastily I turned on the power and watched the dial, expecting to see it record an instant lessening of the undesirable effect. But no apparent change was visible for more than half an hour, when I perceived that the needle had withdrawn very slightly.

---

*Haworth had a most ingenious device for controlling this factor of electric potential. A series of large vacuum tubes emitted free electrons, either into the air of our cabins or into outer space, as the necessity might be. This was not automatically controlled, since we had absolutely no knowledge of probable conditions previous to our actual flight.

After a moment's hesitation, I called Haworth's attention to this phenomenon. He came over and looked at the dial in silence a full minute. Then he began to laugh. The needle had dropped quite perceptibly by this time and Haworth's laughter seemed a signal for the tension of my skin to loosen. It cleared the air, so to speak. Mason looked up doubtfully and, evidently embarrassed by his former conduct, did not speak. But Haworth strode over to him.

"Sorry," he said. "It's not anybody's fault, old man The sun has been pouring free electrons into us for days and we have been building up a terrific electric potential. If we were on the earth now, you would see as fine an electric discharge leave this ship as ever left a thunder-cloud!"

It was good to see Mason and Haworth sane once more. I must say here that our vacuum tubes were not quite powerful enough. We never attained the proper conditions on our whole trip and a certain nervous tension was always present. Fortunately it was slight.

CHAPTER SIX
Land at Last!

ABOUT the middle of August, or 77 by the ship's clock (77 days after May 26th that is) we began to get actively interested in Venus. Mason started it by noticing that you could see a little detail in the periscope, observed it eagerly— a cloudy, muddled kind of a circle two inches across in the glass.

Mason claimed he could see beautiful women in the white cloud mass. After looking for five minutes in mock interest, I suggested you could see anything if you stared until you got spots on your eyes!

But after a few hours Haworth, who had been busy himself at the other periscope glass, straightened up and announced that we were falling at about five miles a second straight onto Venus.

"I've measured the change in degrees of arc subtended by the planet on the glass," he said. "I think you had better check my figures, Mason. I don't think we will have to worry about reducing speed—but we have to do more than think on that subject. We must know!"

Actual navigation on a pre-figured course in space is not as complicated as it might seem at first glance. The advance figuring of the course is difficult, true, but once in space it is merely a matter of keeping on it. On a permanent chart of the fixed stars are traced the positions of the planets at various arbitrary periods. If the planet does not show in the periscope against the pattern of stars precisely where it should, then you are off your course.

It is immediately apparent how far you err and in which direction.

The remaining dimension depending as it does upon whether your speed is too great or too little must be checked by the apparent diameter of the planet you approach. If, at a given minute, it is too small, then your speed has been insufficient and you must apply power at once. Conversely if it is too large at a calculated moment then you have been going too fast and must turn your ship end to and apply power to retard your speed.

So far our course had been so nearly proper as to warrant practically no manipulation. But our close approach to Venus made it imperative to be more accurate than we had been as to our speed and probable time of arrival. We were slightly behind schedule and five or ten seconds of power was required to overcome this.

It took us ten days to fall.

That was undoubtedly the worst time on the whole trip— that falling. You see, the constant strain was there; and yet beyond calculating our speed every few hours, nothing could be done about it. We would try to read or play cards in the slack moments, but there was always that distracting thought that we were actually falling at great speed to the surface of a new and perhaps inhospitable world. I couldn't sleep more than a few hours at a time.

Venus was by now a glorious sight. Sheer white she gleamed and seemed so near in the periscope that one could almost reach out and seize her. She was in half-phase and the terminator line between light and darkness was pure mother-of-pearl. Soft greens and blues tinged the white side and a royal purple edged the line of night.

One or another of us was constantly at the instrument now, searching eagerly for any signs of a break in the dense cloudy veil. But in vain. We thought, however, that we could detect a definite motion, as though the whole globe were turning before our eyes. Mason became very excited over this and made several calculations. He finally announced that the probable length of the day on Venus was sixty hours.

"Thirty hours solid sleep o'nights, Haworth!"

"I suppose they are agitating for the twenty-hour day down there!"

Of course, we thought of Venus as being "down." We were falling onto her surface, you see. Now and again we realized the speed and vehemence of that falling. I, for one, always stopped looking in the periscope when that feeling came on me. I would pick up a book or get somebody to play cribbage with me, for the thought was not a comforting one!

We went over our apparatus a dozen times every twenty-four hours, I suppose. I know I looked over the guns that often. I got to thinking how many things might happen if we did get safely down on Venus. No telling what sort of beasts might be there. Perhaps there might even be some sort of men or other kind of reasoning being.

We had three Remington repeaters for 32 calibre shells; three Colt automatics using the same sized cartridge, and a demountable machine gun for the same ammunition. There were three double bandoleers, each carrying 200 cartridges. That meant six hundred rounds of hot lead for the "welcoming committee," if any. And there was plenty in reserve in the lockers.

Even ten days must pass if you wait long enough, as the Irishman said. But though we haunted that periscope glass the whole time we could not make out one single detail of the planet below us nor could we see a single thing except white and gray clouds. Venus was now a huge disk filling half the heavens.

It was 23:40—89 when Mason called out suddenly from the glass, "Come here quickly! We're almost in the clouds!"

Haworth happened to be in his cot in the other cabin and he leaned over to the duplicate glass beside him and stared a moment.

"Come on in, you two," he shouted. "Landing maneuvers start at once!"

We hurried through to the after cabin and climbed into our cots.

Haworth had protruded our wings in the few seconds' interval and evidently we were already in the rarer outer portions of the atmosphere, for there was a definite pressure toward the nose of the vessel that swung our cots bottoms up that way. Mason was twisting away at the periscope to keep it pointed toward the surface of Venus and Haworth was turning the rudder lever for steering in atmosphere. I glanced at the instrument board and saw that it was again functioning. We appeared to be speeding along at a height of 150 miles, parallel to the surface of the world—but at the fearful speed of six miles a second!

Haworth was quite cool.

"That does it," he said at last. "We should be all right now. We must circle the planet until we lose some of this speed. It will take perhaps seven hours to land. We have to keep wide awake every second of that time."

"Mason, you manage that periscope and keep trying to see some detail. I'll handle the ship."

"And what will I do?"

"Well," put in Mason, smiling but grim-lipped, "what do you think you ought to do about it?"

So I climbed down to the locker and got out drinks for them both.

"She's flying away a bit," I warned Haworth after glancing at the altitudinometer, which now read 175 miles and was slowly climbing.

"I've caught it already. I'm depressing all the wing surfaces to hold her in the atmosphere."

THE dial started to move down again until it reached 120, where it stopped. Then for an hour there was little change. Slowly the altitude dropped and the airspeed indicator with it, as the outside air friction on our hull slowly reduced our speed.

"Free orbit," said Haworth, and he turned the elevator controls the other way. "Now we are navigating just the same as an airplane. Our speed will gradually reduce itself until the wings are required to keep us from falling. From then on it will be simple—merely glide down as slowly as we can and land on the surface."

The next few hours were monotonous. The periscope glass showed nothing but white swirling vapor—a world of fog. The altitude and speed slowly continued to drop. "Seventy-five miles from the surface," I said, reading the indicator.

"That doesn't mean a thing," said Mason. "Not on Venus. Temperature, air pressure, even the gravity is changed. It was designed for the Earth's atmosphere only. Don't bother with it any more now—we're navigating by direct sight."

His eyes remained, while he spoke, riveted on the glass as if his life depended upon it.

At exactly 6:24 Mason gave an inarticulate cry. I leaned over and saw past his shoulder the glass of the periscope. Sure enough, something dark showed beneath the thinning vapors. Was it land or water?

"This is getting too risky," said Haworth tensely. "I'm afraid if we don't get any visibility in the next few minutes we'll have to call the visit off and put on power again for the return to Earth."

(Mason had laid out a course in case of this eventuality.)

But Mason and I had both seen something that time. About a hundred yards beneath us were the tossing billows of a black and somber sea!

I glanced at the instruments.

"Speed 300 miles an hour," I called out.

I looked at the glass to see the water rushing up at us. There was a sudden lurch as Haworth put on our emergency retarding rockets and a great splash obscured the screen. The *Asteroid* bounced violently, jerking us roughly in our cots. Then everything seemed to turn topsy-turvy in the cabin and we swung crazily in response. The floors became walls—the walls were now floors.

Everything was still again except for a slight rolling motion of the ship as she rode the waves. We three looked at each other in an awed manner.

"We're there!" said Mason and laughed doubtfully.

My head was in a whirl of emotion—joy and curiosity uppermost. We were on Venus. Beyond the air lock doors lay the wonders and mysteries of a strange planet.

I was first man out of his cot. I stamped my feet doubtfully, for the full gravity of Venus was pulling now—almost the same as that of Earth. After many weeks of existence at a weight of 80 pounds I now weighed 170. Mason was soon beside me and with a shout of joy fell upon the periscope glass and tried to view the new world outside. But that proved futile. Nothing but steam and spray could be seen. We had been several minutes at the glass when we looked about us and missed Haworth.

Then I saw him down at the provision closet. He had set three glasses on the locker and beside each he was methodically setting out bottles! It was an idea to be hailed with enthusiasm and Mason literally fell on his neck. We were enormously excited and the stimulant seemed to have no effect whatsoever upon us. So we continued drinking the apparently harmless fluids until...well, speaking for myself, I don't remember when we fell asleep. We had been under severe strain for many hours; our expedition had proved entirely successful; here we were landed on the surface of Venus—all very strong mitigating circumstances, as the lawyers say.

According to the clock we slept seven hours. It seemed less than a minute when Haworth awakened us with that best of all alarm clocks—the smell of bacon and coffee. We rose and squandered some of our hoarded water in a good wash all around and sat down to our meal.

"The next thing, of course," said Haworth, "is to see if we can breathe the atmosphere outside."

I made the trip for testing samples. It meant wearing a diving suit, for we dare not expose ourselves even for an instant to what might have been poisonous gases. I had tried a suit on before leaving the earth, but I was by no means accustomed to wearing it. I felt as if I were drowning when I drew in the air contained in the helmet. (Panicky feeling, rather.) But I was so impatient to rush out that I didn't think of any discomforts this time. Mason unscrewed the inner air lock door for me and I squeezed into the closed vestibule. The door shut tightly behind me and I opened the outer door.

Through the glass of my helmet I looked over a foggy ocean. The glass was so obscured with steam and spray that I could make out no details. I had two vacuum jars, one for air and one for water. I found it hard climbing down those rungs in my clumsy dress. I reached the surface of the water and broke the neck of the first jar beneath it, the waves licking up at me as I clung there. It certainly looked like ordinary water.

BACK in the vestibule again, I knocked off the neck of the second jar and stopped it up with the gum Haworth had given me for that purpose. Then I was inside and getting out of the cumbrous helmet by myself—Haworth and Mason (selfish brutes!) eagerly rushing the jars to the little built-in laboratory in the pump room.

By the time I got untangled and over to them they were talking to each other excitedly.

There passed several minutes of tense expectancy.

Suddenly Mason cried out and danced madly about in a circle.

"We can breathe it!" he shouted.

"You can't exactly call it air. There's no nitrogen in it—at least so little as to be not easily detected."

He turned to Haworth excitedly. "Helium!" he explained.

Haworth paused in his own analysis and looked up interested.

"Almost three-quarters helium and the rest oxygen. But it's breathable, just the same—good, life-giving air for all purposes. I'm so certain of it that I don't believe we have to make any more tests!"

Eager as we were to look out and breathe the atmosphere of this new world, yet we waited for our leader to complete his tests on the water. Finally he straightened up, rubbing his forehead with the back of his hand.

"Something queer here. It seems to be H20, but it's full of chlorine. Now why chlorine? Oh, of course! There's not sufficient sodium on Venus to combine with it to make salt as it did on Earth. We'll have to evaporate all water before drinking, anyway. Smelly stuff, isn't it?"

But almost before his remarks were finished he was at the door—eager as any of us. We had both air lock doors open within ten seconds and looked out over the ocean. We breathed recklessly of the air. The breeze was deliciously fresh, full of the taint of chlorine as it was. We could not see far at first for the swirling steam. Water in all directions—not blue or green, but black and rather depressing. The motion and sound of the waves were tremendously exhilarating after our months of utter stillness.

"If this fog would only lift, perhaps we could see something!"

Minute after minute went by. I stared with beating heart at the seascape, such of it as we could see through the whitish vapor. It was another world. The feel of the air, the appearance of the waves, the smell on the breeze and even something additional (perhaps the slight increase in air pressure our instruments recorded) all bespoke the unfamiliar.

After ten minutes peering through the blinding fog Haworth cleared his throat.

"Suppose this fog never does clear!"

A wild thought and great impatience possessed me.

"But if it doesn't, then we can never see anything—never discover anything! Besides, why shouldn't it clear?"

But I realized then, deep inside of me. For centuries the astronomers on Earth had gazed at this planet and never once could they say for certain they had seen anything but clouds. We knew that. Yet we never thought of such a dense fog as this. It was hot mist—in fact, steam. Our faces were wet with water and perspiration, for it was uncomfortably warm out there, in spite of the breeze.

"Well," observed Mason, "just what were you planning to do on Venus when you did get there, Haworth?"

And he smiled ruefully.

We went back inside and ate our meal. We were all of us bitterly disappointed. Our eager sense of adventurous discovery was dampened by too much fog. It was really a terrific letdown. What was to be done?

Haworth, however, had a plan as usual.

"We must find land. Perhaps the mists lessen near land. Certainly, if we can find elevated sections of country we shall be able to climb out of these vapors. We can turn on the power and away we go over the waves! A high-powered speed boat, if you understand what I mean.

"We'll cruise about until we either find land or until our two weeks are up—one or the other."

Our feelings revived considerably, Mason insisted on drinking a toast to Venus and since we had finished our meal he thought brandy appropriate. We three raised our glasses joyfully to the world of new adventure.

"After all," Mason pointed out, "we are sure to strike land soon. We'll leave the *Asteroid* and form a land expedition. On some mountainside or on a high plateau we will find ourselves in clear air and can look around upon our new domain. Think of it!"

He sat staring blindly at his glass and speaking half to himself:

"Think of it... Men on Venus! There she lies outside, the unknown."

He looked up at me suddenly.

"What are we doing here, wasting time? Come! Let's start," and he rose excitedly to his feet.

That was all very well. But there were other things to ascertain.

"We must find our points of the compass," I objected, "or we won't know where we are going."

For answer he brought out a pocket compass.

"Of course it may be off true north, with all the metal there is on this ship, but since there's approximately the same metal in all directions, it may be somewhere near right. There's north, over there."

BUT that did not help much. There was nothing anywhere but oceans. Mason looked out through the open air lock doors.

"Well," he said in mock seriousness, "that makes it an east wind. And sure enough, here comes the rain! We'd better shut the door."

He suited his actions to his words and, returning, sat down again.

"First we will sleep and then we start," Haworth decided.

We slept for eight hours and, upon waking, I noticed in the periscope that the light was about the same as it had been. Did it never grow dark on Venus? I wondered. I called Mason's attention to it.

"Hmmm! Doesn't prove anything. If the atmosphere is as dense as it seems to be there probably is never any real bright day or any absolutely dark night. I think a day is about thirty hours up here."

Subsequent observations tended to confirm his opinion.

After a meal we climbed into our cots and Haworth pulled the starting lever down very gently a few notches only.

It was no motionless feeling this time. The ship bounced and jerked like any sea-borne craft and in the glass I could see the waves sweeping past, one occasionally splashing up over the lens and obscuring all vision until the water dripped off.

"Suppose we hit a rock," I suggested.

Haworth nodded and pushed back the lever a notch or two. The ship, which had been almost horizontal, straightened up until the floors and walls both sloped at a 45-degree angle to our swinging cots. The glass remained clear now, for the nose of the vessel was well above the waves. The speed indicator stood just below thirty miles an hour. We kept steadily on a course due west (if our compasses were accurate). We were proceeding on the theory that on the Earth, at least, the great continent masses ran north and south and we hoped by traveling west we would be more likely to find land.

From time to time Mason went into the vestibule and threw the lead to take a sounding. But the ocean was evidently a very deep one. We proceeded with confidence. Hour after hour went by. I relieved Mason at the glass and he spent his time calculating that at this rate we would circumnavigate the new world in something under a month. The voyage became monotonous. There was one thing settled, however, a very apparent change in the intensity of daylight was noticed by all of us, although it was not by any means real day or night as we knew them on earth. What might be called a slight lessening of the gloom occurred once in about thirty hours. That made Venus' rotation period just what Mason had suggested—sixty hours. I mourned that we had no light measuring instruments in our supplies, with which to check up on these rough observations, but the figure may be taken as probably correct.

But day or night made very little difference to us—for the fog continually shut us in anyway. We stood watches of four hours each, two of us being always on the look out. We drove the ship for nine solid days—6,480 earthly miles by dead reckoning. Then we saw a bird.

Mason saw it, to be precise. He called to us, but it had flown out of focus and he tried in vain to find it again. I urged that we reduce our speed to the point where one of us could stand at the open vestibule and make actual observations as we proceeded.

"We may be getting near land. That bird is a sign of it."

This was agreed to, and I stood the first vestibule-watch. The first thing I did was to take our lead on the end of a long thin line and make soundings, for Mason had not done so in some hours. I found sixty feet of water!

That gave us pause, because even with our huge first step discarded in space, our total length was 110 feet and we drew about 50 of it below the surface.

"The fact is," said Mason, "that we've been absurdly lucky. We might have hit bottom any time the past week. We might have landed this ship on a hard, cold mountain peak to begin with. Let's not tempt fate any further, but take it easy for a while!"

We made a bare ten miles an hour after that, and it was two hours later that I saw a bird. But it was no such bird as I had ever seen before. There was something familiar, though, about the long jagged beak and the great membranous wings. And then I understood.

"Good God! It's a pterodactyl!"

Since we later saw several of these strange flying reptiles, I am in a position to say here that there were certain important differences between the species we observed and those once plentiful upon our own Earth in the Carboniferous Era. But essentially there could be no doubt that the relationship was extraordinarily close. In fact, there were later observed no less than seven reptiles as well as half a hundred insects and vegetable forms of life that could unquestionably be related to current or primitive life forms on Earth. So much so that I am confident the whole theory of the origin of life will, upon closer reasoning, be vastly expanded beyond its present scope.

This is not a scientific paper, however.

Haworth looked up at me from the pump room controls as I announced my find. And just at that moment the ship gave a slight lurch and tipped slowly sideways. Haworth grabbed the power lever and shut off the rockets. Mason started to climb over toward me, while I clung onto the walls of the vestibule and peered out.

There was a blackness a few hundred feet ahead, showing through the surrounding clouds of steam. It could mean only one thing—we had found land!

CHAPTER SEVEN
Adrift in the Fog

OUR first concern was for our vessel and we found she was in water a little less than 47 feet deep. While this was less than we required to be afloat, we were not in the least alarmed. We could, with a small fraction of our rocket power, readily free ourselves. In fact, Haworth decided to go still farther ashore. He turned on the power gingerly while we crept and careened along for another fifty feet. Here, however, the water shoaled rapidly and he shut off the rockets.

There was no question about what to do next. Our cramped quarters made us long to stretch our legs on solid earth once again. There was nothing to delay us. The collapsible boat was lowered and we climbed down into her and pulled for the dark mass of shore showing clearly now through the mist. It was distant about two hundred feet, and when we pulled up alongside it proved to be a mud-bank enormously overgrown with vegetation. Roots, branches and tree-trunks were tangled to the very edge of the water. But do not think there was any familiarity in its appearance. No friendly green leaves met the eye. All was sickly, dirty gray, and such leaves as there were seemed to be mere rudimentary spikes and fronds.

We rowed slowly along this bank, wide eyed and with beating hearts. It was not a friendly land, evidently—but it was outlandish and of exceeding interest.

It was evident from here, however, that higher ground lay to the right. We rowed about two hundred feet through the fog to a shadow, which proved to be a low line of rocks that cropped out through the vegetation.

Haworth pulled the nose of our boat up to them and Mason and I leaped out. We were the first to set foot on the soil of Venus. Haworth announced that he would stand by the boat for five minutes.

"Then one of you must come back," he added, "and give me a chance."

We both carried rifles, of course. At first we could see nothing but mist and hear nothing but the splash of the waves against the rocks. These extended inland, slowly rising, as far as we could see (which was less than 100 yards) and were almost completely bare of vegetation. On both sides of this stony strip lay the steaming, impassable jungle. We took a few hesitant steps and peered about us.

Then I jumped. Something, indistinct in the swirling vapor, ran quickly across from right to left. It was about three feet in height and ran on its two hind legs. There could be no doubt that it had a tail, for this appendage had seemed to be as big as the rest of the animal put together.

We threw our rifles forward and waited expectantly.

Then in the jungle on our right commenced an enormous splashing and crackling of branches. We turned to stare an instant. We both saw something, but could not make it out at first. Then I perceived that it was an enormous neck, huge and shadowy, at the end of which was an absurdly small head.

We retreated hastily to the boat, where Haworth was anxiously endeavoring to see what had caused the noise. We had scarcely got in the boat and pushed off a few feet from shore, when a huge beast slumped out on to the rocky ledge and ponderously crossed it, disappearing into the vegetation on the left.

The beast closely resembled the now extinct earthly species—*Dinosaur brontosaurus*. Of course there were differences. The jaws were long and narrow, almost like a beak, and the legs were longer and thicker than would be indicated by the fossil remains If the brontosaurus lizard. It was a monstrous specimen—easily a hundred feet in length.

But mere words can give no idea of the thrill of proximity to that mountain of flesh. We used the oars frantically to get the boat well away from possible danger. A thousand wild surmises coursed through my brain. First a Pterodactyl and now a dinosaur! Was all this some fantastic nightmare? Were three sane twentieth century humans really set down in some grotesque revival of the Carboniferous Era? My heart was pounding frantically and I noticed Haworth was breathing harder than usual. When the great reptile finally splashed out of sight in the gray-white tangle I breathed a sigh of relief.

"How would you like to get stepped on by that fellow?" asked Mason.

"He is probably too slow to be dangerous," I replied. "An active man could dodge him without breathing hard. And he hasn't more than a few ounces of brain in that tiny head, either. If that's the worst Venus has to show we needn't worry much."

"The real danger on Venus," said Haworth mournfully, "is this damn fog. I should have foreseen it! I think we had better get back to the *Asteroid* and plan out this expedition a little more."

As usual, he was right. This blinding atmosphere was the one thing we had not counted on. It was almost impossible to go anywhere or do anything. You can have no idea (unless you live in London, perhaps) what it feels like to be always unable to see even a clear hundred yards ahead. Beyond that point everything is lost in swirling mist, even when a breeze is blowing. Occasionally the fog blanket shuts down until it is hard to see two steps in any direction.

Just the few yards we had pulled up the shore had taken us completely out of sight of the ship. We found her again, all right, by dead reckoning. But as Mason pointed out:

"Supposing we had gone for a walk on shore and got out of sight of the water?"

"What we should have brought is a bloodhound," I said. "Then we could go where we please and let the dog lead us back."

We sat around our meal in the living cabin and discussed the problem. We had only four days remaining before it would be necessary to start back. And any delay, supposing we had a later course calculated (which we hadn't) made the return trip "more difficult and less desirable," as Mason put it. This was on account of the position of the two planets, Earth and Venus, in their orbits.

We had our compass for direction and our guns for protection, although they might not be much use against such a beast as we had seen. And the compass was not reliable, from having been so long in the enormous metallic hull of the *Asteroid*. Definite aberrations were noticeable in its needle.

"And besides," said Mason, "conditions may be different here as to magnetic fluctuations, even if the compass were trustworthy."

"What we might do," said Haworth thoughtfully, "is to take along a number of stakes and peg one down every hundred feet or so of our progress. Then we could find our way back by them."

One thing we all agreed upon was the desirability of making some sort of expedition. It would be too ridiculous to come all this distance just to see some water and a little jungle!

I was enormously excited at the significance of the beasts we had seen. What vast possibilities it all opened up! It has been suggested by some scientists that life may have arrived on earth out of space in microscopic form. A dust of microbes, perhaps—each capable of undergoing evolution. After all, Venus and Earth were sisters, born of the same sun. Why should not some forms of life grow in parallel directions on both planets? These questions so interested me that I believe I would have cheerfully tramped off into the fog by myself. Probably I should have regretted it bitterly enough if I had, as I was to learn.

OUR conference broke up with the understanding that we would get a few hours' rest and then explore along the rock ledge as far as we could, taking every precaution possible against losing our direction.

That night was the most uncomfortable I ever spent. We had been in the custom of leaving the air lock doors open while traveling over the sea and we did not close them now. But, close to land as we were, the heat was soon unbearable. Bathed in perspiration and unable to sleep, I finally rose and climbed up to the pump room floor (now above us almost vertically) to shut the doors. I believe the action saved our lives.

I had just turned on all the refrigerators and adjusted the oxygen feed and artificial atmosphere controls and was starting to descend to my cot when Haworth screamed.

I glanced hastily down and saw him half risen in bed, battling wildly with both hands, while two bird-like things poised and darted about him. I could see even in that instant a thin trickle of blood that ran from a wound in his cheek. While I stared, I felt something brush my shoulder and, with an involuntary cry, I loosened one hand from its grip on the water-tank rungs and struck at the thing that was attacking me.

None of us had weapons on hand, since these were kept above in the pump room. Our attackers were persistent, so that it was necessary to strike them away with our bare hands. There seemed to be dozens of them. I was in an awkward position, with only one hand free, and when I felt two or three bites deep in my flesh, (one just missed taking out my right eye) I was desperate.

Suddenly the attacks became slower and slower. I couldn't understand why. In an instant I found myself no longer menaced. I felt stronger, too, and breathless from the heat of the struggle as I was. I realized finally that the refrigerators must in some way have turned the trick.

Below me Mason and Haworth were having a breathing spell also. As I looked down at them I saw Haworth slump queerly in a heap on his coat.

Mason and I rushed to him and I got some water from the tank to bathe his face, for he was covered with blood and perspiration. We kept looking warily around for the bird-like things as we worked over him, but saw no signs of them.

Haworth came to his senses after a few minutes and smiled weakly at us.

"Close thing, that!"

We had first aid material in plenty and bandaged each other as well as we could. The wounds were curiously even and neat. A piece of flesh was taken out about one inch long and a quarter of that in width and depth. It was the same in every case. Haworth had one taken out of his chin—black whiskers and all. He had eight such wounds, but Mason and myself were not half as badly off. Unless we had been poisoned, they were nothing serious, we thought.

"We must find those things and kill them," said Mason fiercely, now armed with a frying pan from the kitchen cabinet.

But I would not let him start on the hunt until I had turned on the emergency refrigerator full tilt and the ship, after the stifling Venus temperature, seemed like an icebox.

We found seven of them—helpless and motionless on the floor in the lowest corner. Evidently the cold was beyond their powers of adaptability. They were from nine to twelve inches long and probably insects. I have one specimen with me now and I expect the entomologists will have some trouble deciding its classification, for it has five segments in its body. The remarkable feature is the sharp, powerful beak. It resembles the mandibles of a turtle. Mason smashed all seven thoroughly. But the three we found on the pump room floor above I attended to myself and, as I have said, I kept one specimen intact (but very thoroughly dosed with cyanide of potassium, you may be sure.)

We slept like logs for the next twelve hours and when I awoke my first thought was for my wounds, for I feared poisoning. They were, I was glad to find, perfectly healthy and had already started to heal.

I do not know why I should have feared poison or inoculation of harmful bacteria. I have since given some consideration to the possible bacterial life on Venus. I believe a case might be made out to the effect that harmful bacteria undergo evolution like all other forms of life. Why not? And if that be so, then primitive bacteria such as we were likely to find here might be as harmless in comparison to our modern species on Earth as a gibbon monkey throwing coconuts is, compared to a twentieth century human shooting a rifle. I offer this for what it may be worth—probably very little, for we attempted absolutely no microscopic work on Venus. I have in our collections, however, some dozen vacuum bottles filled with Venus air taken at different levels and locations. Competent scientists will have, at least, some actual data to go on.

But Haworth was still weak and, short as our time was, we must perforce delay our exploration. As it happened, it was nearly forty-eight hours before he felt strong enough. And we felt even then that he only professed his health in order to avoid disappointing us. We wouldn't let him out for another twenty hours.

We sat in the vestibule looking over at the dark shadow that was the shore and discussing the chances of a visit from more of the "mosquitoes" (as Mason was pleased to call them). Mason and I would have made a short trip alone, but we had by this time begun to realize that only with the exercise of the utmost precaution could we hope to make any expedition successful. Haworth was our natural leader and without him we seemed bereft of confidence.

It was just thirty hours before our scheduled return when he insisted we make the venture.

"I'm perfectly all right now," he said, "and we have to act right away or probably never get the chance again."

He seemed strong enough, although his face was paler than usual, perhaps. We gathered our equipment—some food, rifles, bandoleers, two hatchets and the compasses— and Haworth followed us down the ladder, first closing the air lock door and leaving the key in the slit.

"We might lose the key if we took it with us," he explained.

I rowed. We went as before, directly to the mud-bank and along it to the ledge of rock, where we disembarked. Mason had brought along a length of line and he tied one end to a broken piece of rock. The other end was fastened to the nose of our little boat, which he pushed strongly out from the shore, heaving the rock after it. She swung jauntily at her mooring, about twelve feet off shore.

"Just so one of your giant lizard friends doesn't step on her," he grinned at me. "We can easily get out to her at that depth."

Our compass was consulted and due north seemed to be about in the direction we had left the *Asteroid*. The opening between the jungle-swamps on either hand seemed to lead away to the east.

"First," said Haworth, "we must get some stakes to set out as we go."

He went to the edge of the rock and hacked away, Mason helping him, at some of the plants in the jungle's rim. They cut branches about four feet long and, as the wood was spongy and easily severed, the labor was inconsiderable. We soon had a dozen stakes apiece and Haworth drove the first one into a natural crack in the rocks.

Then we picked up our bundles of sticks and our rifles and proceeded eagerly into the mist. I was wildly excited. Every step might bring us into sight of something new. Most certainly it would be "unearthly." We walked as quietly as we could, for no telling what danger might lurk around us. Eager as we were, I don't think we could have been called comfortable in our minds. From the right we could hear distant sounds of splashing and from both sides of the jungle life was audible in faint rustlings and indistinct sounds.

When we had gone about a hundred yards, we fixed another stake upright with loose stones. As we moved along, the ledge of rock widened, until we could no longer see even the shadow of vegetable growth on each side. The ground sloped gently upward as we progressed.

We were adrift in a sea of fog.

MASON gasped and gripped my arm tensely. He was staring to the right and following his line of vision I saw an amorphous mass loom darkly against the gray steam. We stood stock-still for a minute—scarcely breathing. Then Haworth whispered:

"It doesn't move. Let's get a little nearer."

Very cautiously we did so. It was a tree.

Vastly relieved, we approached and found three trees growing close together in a pocket of earth which lay like an oasis in this fog-bound desert of rock. They were curious trees, about fifty feet in height and clothed with foliage at the top only. The trunks were faintly suggestive of certain tropical tree ferns I had seen in greenhouses in New York, but of course by no means the same. Every foot or so the bark ended in a curious sort of protruding knob, flattened on its upper surface. Behind each knob an inner layer of bark continued up the trunk, to curl outward a foot higher in the same sort of thing. I put out my hand and found the projections very hard and, to my surprise, strong enough to bear my weight.

"This would be mighty convenient to climb if we meet any desperate characters!" I remarked jocularly.

"Hsssssh!"

Mason was holding his head in a strained listening attitude. Haworth was holding his finger to his lips and I strained my ears expectantly. Unconsciously we drew together close to the trunk of one of the tree ferns.

I saw something move. It was just a shadow at first. Then I could see that it walked on two legs. As it came still closer I could distinguish arms and claw-like hands. It was about three feet high. Its face was mostly snout and teeth, but in one of the hands it held a tree branch crudely broken off to form a club!

Curious sliding steps it took—straight toward us. At about fifty yards distance it stopped suspiciously and stared in our direction, as if hesitating whether or not to come further.

Haworth pressed my shoulder warningly and then slowly advanced out of the shelter of the trees. He moved with the utmost precaution "to avoid frightening it," as he afterwards explained. But he need not have worried had he known as much about the courage of these animals as we did a little later on.

The creature remained motionless until he had advanced twenty feet. Then it stirred nervously. Haworth came to a halt and raised his right arm slowly over his head. There was no motion from the other and Haworth started to talk to it in a quiet tone of voice. I could see the head twitch suddenly at the sound, but there was no other response.

Then Haworth took another step forward and like a flash the creature spun about and fled in great leaping strides.

Our leader shouted at it excitedly and followed. We, in turn, followed Haworth. We ran about a hundred yards when we came in sight of a dense growth of trees. We were panting painfully and absolutely saturated with sweat in that hothouse atmosphere.

"Did you see the club? That means an opposing thumb on the hand! There isn't any doubt the beast is intelligent to at least some extent!"

"This is the most important thing we have seen yet."

But I had seen something of a different sort when beast had turned to flee.

"It has a tail," I reminded them. "A real large tail, almost as big as a kangaroo's. And that snout strongly suggests the reptile, if ever I saw one!"

We walked slowly toward the dark shadow of the forest, mopping our brows and endeavoring to recover our breath. The ground here was possibly fifty feet higher in elevation than the swamps at the water's edge and the growth of vegetation was not nearly so rank as it was down there.

Openings were visible here and there between the tree-trunks.

We were within fifty feet of one opening when we all three stopped uncertainly, as though we had realized in unison that danger might lie hidden just behind that screen of foliage. And as we stood there I saw a movement in the shadows, close to the ground. Out from the woods stepped the animal we had been pursuing and beside him stood half a dozen more of the same kind. Slowly they came out into the open. Still more of them followed and spread out on each side until nearly fifty of the beasts were visible.

We all three had dropped our bundles of stakes and had our rifles ready for action.

"Don't shoot until we have to," whispered Haworth and stepping forward a pace he raised his rifle in the air and gestured with his free arm.

"There, there, there," he said in a soothing tone. "We'd like to be friends if you'd let us."

They seemed undecided as to how they would take this. They cocked their heads sideways, some of them, for all the world like a dog that has been spoken to. Two or three of them uttered curious little croaks and shifted uneasily on their feet. I was beginning to believe we might establish some sort of understanding with them after all, when one of the beasts began leaping up and down and uttering wild chattering squeals. At that they all seemed to get excited and started to advance upon us.

I raised my rifle and pulled the trigger, aiming at the foremost of the creatures, which slumped to the ground and lay there thrashing his tail and biting savagely at the rocky ground.

The shot stopped them.

It rang out like a thunderclap on the still air. The whole of Venus seemed to be standing still and listening in wonder at the strange sound. But without a pause Mason and Haworth stepped forward, guns ready. I followed suit.

"We've got to bluff them and keep 'em bluffed," Mason whispered.

We never knew how it might have turned out. There was a brisk crashing away on our left and we swung in that direction. The sounds were approaching, but we could see nothing as yet. In that brief second the whole group of reptile-men disappeared. Only the dead one lay on the ground when we turned back. What was this thing approaching us that caused them to flee?

"Let's get out of here quick!"

CHAPTER EIGHT
Desperate Moments

WE followed Haworth down the slope at a trot. We were out of breath instantly in the terrible heat and dampness and when the clump of three trees showed itself through the mist we paused to gather ourselves together. Behind us we heard the crashing now much closer. Suddenly a huge coughing roar shook the very ground we stood on.

"Quick!" I shouted. "We can get up these trees and be safe!"

The sounds were coming nearer now with terrifying rapidity as we all three started up the ladder like trunk of the nearest tree fern. We climbed as far as we could—about forty feet—and looked down with pounding hearts.

Suddenly there burst into view a huge beast running at a terrific pace. He strode gigantically on two hind legs, holding his fore feet under his chin. Most terrifying of all were his great jaws—fully six feet in length and massively armored with gigantic teeth.

I recognized a startling resemblance to that most ferocious and powerful living creature ever known to the human race— the great *Dinosaur tyrannus Rex!*

He must have winded us as he passed the tree, for he came to a grinding stop just beyond us, his huge talons making long grooves in the eroded surface of the rock. Then he wheeled fiercely and bounded back to rear his thirty-foot height up at us.

We were in the palm-like top of the tree by now, as you may imagine, and hanging on for dear life. The shock of his great weight almost did for me. My hold loosened as the tree sprang back from the blow and I slipped down half-a-dozen feet until my tearing, bleeding fingers got a grip again. I scrambled back to my place again in a panic.

The terrific beast seemed to realize we were beyond his reach, for he did not again make an attempt to seize us. His great slavering jaws opened to emit a huge blasting roar and he made off back toward the woods, where he intended doubtlessly to dispose of the reptile-man I had shot.

The last roar was accompanied by a wet scorching stench such as I hope never again to experience. I was nearly sick at the first whiff of it and could not bear to draw breath until the slight breeze had made the air possible once more.

We could hear the beast at its grisly meal, although he was several hundred feet distant and entirely invisible. In twenty minutes back he came and his little eyes stared up at us coldly. He stood there a few minutes and then moved off and we could hear him grunting and snorting as he forced his way through the woods up the slope.

We three were completely prostrated. You have no notion how enervating climate can be. I could laugh at our worst earthly tropics after what I have been through! Even a slow walk started the perspiration running in torrents and we had been running and scrambling for our very lives. Our nerves were frayed, too. And poor Haworth was barely able to hold on to his branch. In fact, we fixed a sort of couch up there for him and he sprawled on it, his neatly pointed beard now in filthy disarray. I managed to slip down to the ground, taking it slowly, and pick up one hatchet and two rifles. The other hatchet had been dropped and one of the rifles had been stepped on by our perfumed visitor. With the hatchet we chopped some of the great leaves and wove them across two branches. Haworth fell asleep almost immediately and Mason and I talked over things worriedly.

"I'd judge we're about five hundred yards from shore," said Mason. "If we strike it right, that would be easy. We'd better start as soon as Haworth can move."

We consulted the compass and decided upon the general direction, which was west, naturally. We had borne almost due east when we started off from the boat. But direction meant nothing tangible in that blinding mist. We estimated we ought not to be two hundred yards from the nearest stake.

"Why shouldn't one of us start down and scout around," I suggested, "while the other stays here with Haworth?"

"All right. I'll go, if you like."

But I insisted on making the trip myself. I climbed down and started off due west by compass. I moved in absolute silence, gun in the crook of my arm. We had agreed that in case of alarm Mason was to start calling from the treetop and that I could quickly find my way back guided by his voice.

After I had walked what I guessed to be two hundred yards I looked carefully about me in the fog, but could see absolutely nothing like a stake anywhere. I spent ten minutes searching over the bare rock without success and started back. After all, I thought to myself, we know the general direction. It should be a simple matter to find the shore again. I felt that I could have proceeded directly to it then and there.

When I had walked back a sufficient distance I was surprised to be unable to see the clump of trees. I didn't dare to call out for God knows what frightful answer I might receive. But in what direction was I to turn?

That moment was the worst of my life, I fully believe. Alone on a strange and terrible planet. Lost!

I stopped dead still and listened, but either my heart was pounding like a bass drum and drowned out all lesser sounds, or else the swirling mists were without voice. Come, I thought to myself, I must keep my head. There's no use getting into a panic! And of course that made things worse than ever. I tried to observe my own footmarks on the rocks and could trace my steps quite easily for a dozen feet but they were soon obliterated by the wet fog and I gave that method up in despair. Then I started running.

Don't ask me why! I didn't run far, for a worse thought came to me and stopped my course in one wild heart-straining slither. Suppose I were running away from the three trees and got out of range of Mason's voice?

I tried to retrace my steps and got started, at least, in the right direction, walking quietly so as to hear any noise there might be. Then the marks on the dripping rock became indistinguishable and I cast around vainly for a clue, trembling now with the heat and my physical and nervous exhaustion.

I spent another ten minutes of frantic searching over the barren ground when I heard a sound. For one terrible half-second I did not recognize Mason's voice. Then I gasped my relief and ran silently and very wetly towards the voice. I climbed the tree almost as quickly as I had done the first time and Mason patted my shoulder to steady me, for I was trembling in every limb.

"Easy there, lad! Why all the excitement? Get lost down there?"

I TOLD him presently of the extreme difficulty of finding one's way about alone on Venus. The horror of that moment never left me while we remained on the planet. I wished for nothing but a return to the clear atmosphere of our own Earth. As a matter of fact, I was in a plain funk, although for some reason I now find I dislike writing it down as that.

It is nice to think of one's self as a bold heroic figure. (Intrepid explorer, you know.) But sitting here in security as I write, I wonder that I ever had courage enough at first to set foot on the soil of Venus and I realize clearly that I am not at all a brave man. Similarly, I wonder how many African explorers were frightened out of their wits by their first sight of a lion? It's easy to forget such things afterwards, or rather, I should say it is hard to admit them.

Haworth was stirring in his sleep by then and muttering incoherently. I was physically sick from my recent adventure and even Mason was exhausted. It was clearly impossible to do anything at all until we had rested. We had stuffed some food in our pockets before leaving the *Asteroid* and made a light meal in the treetop. For drink, Mason climbed down and filled his hat with the warm steaming water that made shallow puddles in every hollow of the rock. It was not exactly delicious, but at least it was not tainted with chlorine, as was the ocean, for the pools were formed by evaporation and condensation, of course. After that we felt a little better.

By this I do not mean comfortable. We were never comfortable on Venus. Our clothes were always dripping wet with mist and perspiration. Water oozed from our shoes and dripped down our backs and legs. In fact, clothes were not strictly necessary at all. We wore jackets of white duck and trousers of the same, tucked into high boots. The jackets gave us handy pockets; the trousers and boots gave protection. We wore no hats or underclothing of any kind.

Haworth slept on, hour after hour, while Mason and myself occupied our time speculating over what we had seen, and observing the life before us. Once a pterodactyl flew past us—his great twenty-foot wings outspread in motionless flight and his long-toothed beak stretched in front of him. He was almost jet black in color and looked leathery. We had a good look at him, for he passed within thirty feet of our tree and did not travel very rapidly. None of these flying reptiles that we observed seemed to flap their wings at all, but depended entirely upon soaring. In fact, their bodies were so small in comparison to their huge wingspread, I doubt that they could move their wings with sufficient force to fly as an earthly bird does.

I had time to observe carefully the tree in which we rested. The leaves were of the compound type and sprang from the main stem on stout three-sided branches, (or possibly leaf stalks). The leaf divided in pectate fashion on both sides, growing narrower toward the tip and ending in a short club-like growth of sticky pink which may have been some rudimentary sort of flower. We could observe several insects on the branches and I captured half a dozen, which I placed in a flat tin specimen box I always carried in my jacket pocket. Two of them were suggestive of exotic forms I had seen pictured in earthly books of entomology.

One was some sort of beetle-like species and the other a kind of "darning-needle" about seven inches in length. The other insects (if they indeed prove to be insects at all) were outlandish looking things. Mostly the colors were varying hues of sickly whites and grays, similar to the foliage.

Once we heard a terrific rumpus start down in the jungle. We supposed that our friend *Tyrannus Rex* had encountered the brontosaurus. We could hear some great tail smacking the surface of the water, if it were brontosaurus, he was evidently not equipped with vocal organs, for the grunting and roaring was all one-sided. So was the battle, evidently. It lasted about ten minutes and our late visitor probably for once in his life had enough to eat for a while. That carcass would have fed a regiment for a week. As the noise ceased, I thought I could see one of the reptile-men moving across the open rock in the direction of the sounds, but it was just far enough away as to be only a vague shadow in the fog. Possibly it was mere imagination.

Then three little running things raced past our clump of trees and out of sight, being presently followed by a long dead-white running creature on eight flimsy legs. He was a nightmare! His body was not more than six inches through and yet was a good six feet in length, with a huge triangular head armed with jaws that kept opening and shutting viciously as he ran. He was out of sight in a moment and we never observed another like him during the time we spent on the planet.

The time dragged slowly. Mason and I occasionally addressed a remark to each other as we watched. He was nervously consulting his watch every little while.

"This may be mighty serious, you know," he said at last. "We have only three hours left now before we will simply have to start back for the ship. We must commence our return flight to the Earth on time or—not at all. A delay means figuring the direction and course out all over again. That may not be possible."

"What! And you such a good astronomer!"

"Oh, it's the time it would take that bothers me. You see, I can't apply a formula to the calculation, because there are three variables. And the trial and error method means a lot of figuring."

"But suppose you do figure out the course all over again, what of it? Suppose we are a week behind schedule, that only means arriving a week late back home, doesn't it?"

Mason looked uncomfortable and very serious.

"I'm afraid not. The schedule was planned to allow the utmost possible time on Venus. If we are delayed, Venus would get too far ahead of the Earth in its course about the sun. We would have to wait over a year before we could find it possible to return."

"Great Heavens! A year in this living Hell?"

"Exactly!" answered Mason and he bent over Haworth with an anxious air.

The full purport of Mason's words began to flow in on me. What would we do? Even supposing we got back safely to the vessel—as of course we must, sometime—what would a whole year be like here? Our food supplies were, of course, entirely inadequate for such a length of time. Our fuel was not inexhaustible and even the slight amount required to keep the refrigerators going could not be spared for a year's operation. I passed my hand over my greasy and dripping forehead and reflected wildly on twelve solid months of unmitigated Venus climate.

We might kill reptiles for food—one moderate-sized brontosaurus would keep us going for months. Stay though! For a few days only, come to think of it. No meat would keep a week in that climate. We would have to kill every other day. Hunting expeditions into that blind blanketing fog! Oh how I longed for one soul filling glimpse of an earthly landscape on a clear crisp autumn day with miles upon miles of rolling country to the hazy horizon!

And suppose the "mosquitoes" attacked us on a hunting expedition? Or *Tyrannus Rex* got on our trail at a distance from the nearest tree? And moreover what new and as yet unencountered monstrosities of nature might lie in store for us farther inland?

MY vague fears and longings to get back to the ship now amounted almost to hysteria. It put out of my mind any fear for what might menace us on the ground below. I fidgeted desperately a few minutes and then suggested that we try to wake our companion and get started along. Mason thought we should wait a little longer but finally shook Haworth's shoulder and called his name. His eyes came open vacantly and he blinked at us weakly for a few seconds.

"We ought to be getting back, old man," I put in. "Do you think you can make it yet?"

"What time is it?"

We told him and explained that there was less than three hours' grace before our scheduled start. He sat up immediately and professed himself well able to move.

"I feel a little dizzy," he confessed, "but I'm all right really."

We climbed down the tree in strict silence and listened carefully and peered in all directions, but there seemed no danger. We scouted about a little and I found the lost hatchet a few dozen yards up the slope. Then we got out Mason's compass and Haworth suggested that Mason start ahead. I was to follow him about a hundred feet behind, while Haworth himself would bring up the rear allowing the same interval between himself and me.

"In that way we can be sure we are at least traveling in a straight line."

We did this and aimed our course due west. But as if to hinder us in every way possible, the breeze had died down and the fog closed on us like a ghostly pall. We found that we had to draw closer together to remain visible to each other. We walked for ten minutes in utter stillness and should have come in sight of either the shore or the jungle, but nothing was to be seen except the uneven surface of the bare rock on which we walked. Mason stopped a moment and we all paused to look carefully about us. Then we continued our walk for ten minutes more. By this time we knew we had definitely missed the seemingly simple route. Haworth closed up towards, me and Mason also started back to join us.

We examined the compass carefully and it certainly seemed an uncertain thing to depend on for our lives. Back on earth it had been a very expensive and reliable instrument. But here it wobbled and pivoted unsteadily over forty-five degrees of the horizon, (Just an earthly simile, for there wasn't such thing as a "horizon," only the white wall of fog shutting us in.)

"We can only keep walking," Haworth worried. "If we keep spreading out this way we will go in a straight line at least and will certainly come to some place in time."

"We were only five hundred yards from the shore when we left those trees," complained Mason. "We knew the general direction. It doesn't seem possible that we have missed a simple course like this."

But we had.

In the next five minutes the ground commenced to slope upward and I knew we were absolutely lost. We kept on, however, for a few minutes more until Mason stopped suddenly, turned toward us and beckoned. We walked quickly and quietly up to where he stood and found ourselves in sight of the line of woods. We moved up closer and came upon signs of a struggle, for there was a good deal of blood about the ground.

I looked about me and thought I recognized the spot where we had encountered the reptile-men. I told the others and, after some hesitation, they both agreed with me. We eyed the dark shadow of the trees, half expecting to see a mob of the creatures pour out to attack us, but everything was quiet and nothing appeared in our range of vision except the motionless trunks with their vague feathered tops.

We at least knew where we were once more and set out at once for the clump of three trees where we had spent so many hours. These were not far away and we found them without much trouble and flung ourselves down to rest beside them. For, as I have said before and again point out, Venus is cursed with an almost inconceivably uncomfortable climate. We had been walking almost half an hour and, personally, I felt as if I had just fallen into a warm lake.

It was fortunate we had found the trees when we did. We had not been there two minutes before we heard *Tyrannus Rex* roaring and crashing about in the distance. Heaven knows what had disturbed him, for he must have made the world's record meal off his enormous victim a few hours ago. We started up at the sounds, all three of us, and were soon in no doubt that he was headed our way. We knew what to do about that by this time, however. Up we went, Haworth first, myself next and Mason last.

Mason surveyed with comical disgust the couch we had built in the top of the tree.

"Home again!" he said ironically.

We could hear the crashing sounds coming nearer and then we suddenly saw several indistinct things moving below us about two hundred feet away. The breeze had sprung up again and visibility was better than it had been. They were reptile-men and there were dozens of them. I could hardly resist crying out to warn them before it occurred to me that they could hear the approaching dinosaur as well as we could. I stared in wonder at the little creatures. They were dragging three long ropes, which seemed (we had a chance to examine them later) made from some kind of climbing vine. Half a dozen were clustered together at the end of each length of rope, which must have been two hundred feet, although it was difficult to be certain of anything in the uncertain mist.

As we watched, they spread out excitedly and two of the ropes were dragged away out of sight. The third one was stretched in a straight line, the reptiles on the near end of it coming right under our tree, but without observing us. Then the main body of reptiles walked forward in a mob towards the approaching monster.

"You don't suppose they can take him into camp!" exclaimed Mason.

Haworth's eyes were shining and his face showed the greatest excitement. I heard him mutter:

"True reasoning animals. If they can fight that fellow, they have conquered their environment and no mistake!"

CHAPTER NINE
Lost

SUDDENLY the great dinosaur uttered a prodigious roar and we heard his crashing twenty-foot strides racing toward us. The mob of reptiles were running for their lives now and crossed over the slackened rope just as the beast burst into view through the fog. He arrived at the rope, in three bounds and the same number of seconds. As he did so, the six reptile-men beneath us heaved on the end of it and it rose a foot or two into the air. Tyrannus caught his foot hard against it and the shock pulled the little struggling group ten feet outwards.

But as for their enemy—!

The vibration of his fall caused even the tree in which we crouched to tremble slightly. He lay there stunned. The creatures beneath us raced at high speed off into the fog, taking their rope with them. Then the great beast scrambled to his feet, roaring again and again as he did so. He looked uncertainly about him and, shaking his head stupidly, suddenly started off into the fog once more at full speed.

In a few seconds we heard again the crash of his second fall. This time he was silent for almost two minutes and in the silence we could distinctly hear the squealing and grunting of his hurrying tormentors.

"Amazing! Perfectly amazing!" whispered Haworth.

Mason was grinning delightedly.

"Aren't they the little dears?" he asked happily. "Now I know I want to make their acquaintance!"

Again we heard the thudding rush and the resounding tumble, but this time the dinosaur was evidently on his feet too soon, for we heard his roaring and two or three high-pitched squeals. Some of the little fellows had been caught.

But there were plenty of them to continue the game, and continue it they did for half an hour—now drawing away from us and now approaching. Finally we were sure they had turned their trick, for five minutes of silence had followed the last crashing fall. As we gazed eagerly in the direction of the last noises, we perceived the reptile-men racing toward us out of the mist.

This time nearly twenty of them crouched beneath our clump of trees, all holding tightly to the end of their rope and staring fixedly out in the direction from which they had come. At the other end of the rope another group could be seen dimly through the fog.

The great coughing roar broke forth afresh and once more the enraged dinosaur came into view. He was not traveling so fast this time, however, and he was covered with blood and filth. His great jaws were wide open and blood of a startling green hue dripped from them.

The rope tightened before his step and tripped him. But this time, while he was still hurtling through the air, the reptile-men rushed out, abandoning their rope. At the same time the other group closed in on him and presently through the white wall that shut us in came a vast mob of them, all racing swiftly toward their now silent foe. Desperately they threw their ropes over his body and twisted them about the slowly moving tail. Some of them carried large rocks and half a dozen at once clambered swiftly up on his back and commenced hammering with the rocks on his spine. It looked as though they had won their battle for a minute, but the end was not yet. Suddenly the great tail swept up into the air with three of the reptile-men clinging to it and crashed down again on the ground. The huge legs began to scramble for a grip on the stone and the dinosaur rose unsteadily to his feet—the creatures on his back still pounding desperately with the heavy rocks. Their victim was shaky, as could readily be observed, but he was by no means finished.

Frantically the ropes were tightened and those immediately in his path attempted to escape, but the huge jaws reached down and crunched heavily on three of them before you could snap your fingers. The beast surged forward, dragging four ropes and a hundred of his tormenters after him.

So far we had carefully remained in the role of observers, but to do so longer was more than human flesh and blood could stand. We had two good rifles left and, as Mason and Haworth scrambled down the trunk, I took careful aim at my mark and fired ten shots as fast as I could pull the trigger. The efforts of the reptile-men to break the beast's spinal column had given me my clue. I had aimed carefully for this apparently vital spot and I am sure I must have hit at least once, for the range was not more than two hundred feet.

As I hastily refilled the cartridge chamber, I saw my two foolhardy companions start out from the foot of the tree. Haworth had his revolver in hand and Mason had the rifle at his shoulder. They fired as I looked and the dinosaur wheeled about, trailing his hundred stubborn followers behind him and made straight for us. I saw my friends start back to the tree and realized in the same instant that they could never get up out of reach in time.

It was up to me. But the great head now completely obstructed my aim at the one vital spot! My mind raced desperately over a dozen possibilities, but finally I determined to aim for his left eye and, raising my rifle, I pumped ten 32-calibre bullets straight into it.

He kept coming forward for half a second and it was not until he crashed down on his breast that I realized his forward motion had been merely falling.

We never did know exactly what killed him. Perhaps my shots in his back had not taken effect until then, or possibly a few ounces of lead in his brain had done the trick. But he did not move again. My companions had got a few feet up the tree trunk and they now descended once more and waited until I had joined them, when we all three walked forward.

The reptile-men had drawn together in a crowd on the other side of the carcass and they eyed us in silence. Haworth prodded the dead dinosaur with his foot and then held his arm in the air in salutation. We raised our arms also, following his lead, and we all three proceeded to make what we considered to be friendly sounds and gestures. I do not recollect what particular words I said, but I could hear Mason repeating over and over again:

"You plucky little beggars! You *plucky* little beggars!"

They cocked their heads at us and one of them whom we had observed during the fight, which he had several times appeared to be directing, stepped forward a few paces and croaked or grunted (it was an indescribable sound) at us. Haworth promptly mimicked him as well as he could and beckoned vaguely with his left hand. The reptile then jumped in the air several times, quite lively, and stood still, staring inquisitively at us.

Haworth turned around to us.

"I'm blessed if I know what to do," he said. "Can you think of any gesture or sound that might be common to both men and reptiles?"

IT struck me at once—we both had to eat! I opened my mouth to its widest and pointed with my right hand down my throat, smacking my lips loudly. The creature stared at me silently for several seconds. Then he turned his head to the body lying beside us and looked back to me again.

"He evidently thinks you ought to eat your kill," said Mason. "Tell him you want him to cut it up and bring it to you on a silver platter!"

But that gave me another idea. I had a knife in the cotton belt of my trousers. Quickly I pulled this out and walked over to the huge head. I stooped down and cut a two-pound piece from the green, drooling tongue. This I held in my outstretched hand and slowly advanced toward the reptile chief.

That saved the day. He let me come right up to him and took the meat with his strange little claw-fingers; put the whole two pounds into his commodious mouth; chewed it twice and swallowed it—holus-bolus!

And then Haworth had an inspiration. He walked up to the carcass of the late *Tyrannus Rex* and made a broad sweeping gesture toward the gathering of reptiles. Then he backed off a pace and repeated his gesture, keeping the performance up until he reached our vicinity. (I had rejoined Mason in the meantime). That apparently settled the doubts of our visitors. There was a mad scramble for the body and such a piece of trencher-work as they made of it! Their long sharp jaws tore great pieces of flesh out and little attempt was made at mastication. They just gulped it down in a hurry and went back for more. Not even the tough hide seemed to interfere with digestion.

We three humans drew off a little to one side. I was too interested to feel disgusted. Several quarrels started here and there and one poor fellow got badly bitten and had to withdraw to attend to his wounds.

But Mason was nervously consulting his watch.

"We have to act quickly to meet our schedule. Do you suppose that you could give them the idea we want to go back where we came from?"

"Not much chance of that for a while yet!"

And indeed the carnival was at its height. We watched in some amusement the gargantuan meal. Then a movement of shadows beyond the feasters caught my eye. I called Haworth's attention to it and we peered anxiously through the mist, hastily reloading our empty guns from our bandoleers. The shadows did not seem to be approaching, but merely hovered in the background and, since the feasters did not appear to be in the least alarmed, we concluded it must be the "second table" waiting their turn. In this surmise we were entirely correct.

The fury of the prandial onslaught waned and presently they climbed off the raw and gruesome carcass by twos and threes—bloody from head to foot and with noticeably distended bellies. Before the last one could get out of the way, figures emerged literally by the hundred from the surrounding fog—many young ones among them—and all that had happened before might be considered polite table manners compared to the scene that now ensued.

"Women and children last!" and Mason turned away. I felt a little squeamish.

"Now is our chance to try and explain to the chief that we need a guide. Things are getting pretty desperate, you know! An hour and a half more delay and it may mean the end of us. Have you any ideas about sign languages?"

It seems strange enough now that we were not more alarmed than we were. Somehow the knowledge that we were only a quarter of a mile from our vessel kept us from getting into a panic. But on Venus, blinded by the swirling steamy air, with an unreliable compass, it might as well have been a hundred miles. We were, however, entirely uncomfortable and weakened in nerve and body as well as being drenched with perspiration from the stifling heat. In addition, as I have said, I myself did not once fully recover from my complete horror and fear while we remained on the planet.

We spent several minutes in deep thought, occasionally interrupted by those incoherent exclamations that accompany the consideration of serious problems. We finally reached an opinion that if Haworth took the chief aside and pointed in the approximate direction and then attempted to start him along with us, the meaning would be clear enough. And so it would, perhaps. But when Haworth approached the group of warriors it was impossible to identify the chief. They were sprawled in all sorts of attitudes upon the rocky ground, licking their bodies with their long pink tongues or blinking vacantly at one another in surfeited delight. But when Haworth got within ten feet of the nearest, up he jumped and stood eyeing him uneasily. He approached another step and they all got up and moved back before him.

And there we were.

So Haworth pointed in a general westerly direction and made huge beckonings with his other arm, but the beasts just blinked stupidly and some of them backed away a step or so more. He called Mason and myself over and we came instantly, rifles ready, but all he wanted us to do was to stand beside him and make the same gestures he did. We pointed and beckoned for a minute and then he whispered:

"Now let's all back away in the direction we want to go."

So we started off slowly, looking over our shoulders. But if any reaction was apparent on the part of the reptile-men it was one of relief. We stood there, uncertain what to do next.

"We haven't another minute to waste," announced Mason firmly, looking at his watch. "Now let's start west in single file as we did before. But this time let's keep going until we reach the shore. Why, the damn thing is only a few hundred yards away!"

So we took a last look at the reptile-men. The warriors were staring silently back at us and the children and females were too busy to pay us any attention whatever. Then we turned about and started off—Haworth in the lead, myself next and Mason (with the compass) bringing up the rear. After fifty steps I turned around and noticed that the mists had swallowed up the scene of the battle completely, although I could readily tell the direction in which it lay by the confused murmur of the feasters. Keeping spaced out one hundred feet or so apart we proceeded over the rocky surface in as straight a line as we could, with due alterations called out by Mason from the rear and based, he afterwards confessed, half upon the compass and half upon his own good guess.

After a while the ground sloped down slightly and through the surrounding white wall of fog on our right a line of shadow appeared. It was the jungle-swamp. I had rather expected that we would sight it, if anywhere, upon our left, but presumably I had been confused in the mists. Presently Haworth stopped and waited until we both joined him.

"We might as well keep together now. We have only to follow the edge of the jungle down to the shore."

"Thank God!" I exclaimed fervently.

But after twenty minute's march, we were not so sure. And then the swamp's edge curved inwards and we were forced to bear to the left to avoid it. The curve continued until we found our course absolutely cut off. We were lost again.

Mason thought a moment.

"We must be on a tongue of rock running out into this sea of jungle, there's no other explanation. Let's go back to where we first hit the edge of this swamp."

I just followed the others blindly, rifle clutched tightly and my teeth clenched so hard together that my jaws were sore for several days afterwards. We cut across and retraced our steps, walking now more quickly than we had done, and soon came to the end of the jungle. Here it bore away to our left. I wanted to follow it (I wish we had) but the others felt sure that our course lay to our right.

"If we turn right here," said Haworth, "and keep going a few minutes without striking the jungle on the other side of this clear space, then we'll go back and try your way."

But my panic made me obstinate and I started off and went perhaps fifty feet along, close to the jungle. Then the figures of my companions dimmed slightly in the surrounding fog and I turned and incontinently rejoined them.

We had not been walking two minutes—keeping as straight as we could in our single file formation—when Haworth waved to us, silently. When we reached him the jungle wall was showing vaguely in the steamy air. We felt hopeful once more.

"It's about time, too! Another twenty minutes and we would have been too late to make it. We'll have to hurry along as it is. I hope the little boat is safe where you left her, Mason."

We had been completely exhausted in the vitiating temperature (how Haworth kept going I do not know) but we forgot our discomforts in this fresh hope. In five minutes the tall shadow of a tree swam mistily in the middle distance. At the same time we became aware of a murmur of sound upon our left.

It was the reptile men still at their feast!

We were back where we had started from. Listlessly we turned to the sound and made our way towards it.

CHAPTER TEN
A Strange Malady

AS we approached our three familiar tree ferns once again, everything was suddenly quiet, and when the advancing wall of mist before us disclosed the gathering of feasters, they were in compact array, eyeing us very uneasily, I thought. We attempted to signal them our wishes, but received no answer except the steady emotionless staring.

Evidently they knew us, for after a moment they turned about and started off for the woods on the slope above. We followed them. You could not say we accompanied them, for not one of the beasts would permit us to come closer than ten or twelve feet. On they kept at a rapid pace until the woods were again in sight, we three puffing and sweating behind them and gesturing and talking like madmen. I question, in fact, if we were any longer entirely sane.

Without a pause the whole party plunged into the forest of tree ferns and we perforce followed. I don't believe we had any definite plan, but we were desperate. It was dark under the foliage, but fairly easy walking. The soil was a mere coating over the rock and the ground was firm to the foot. Several times the reptile-men nearest us (never nearer than ten feet) turned to stare back, but whether from mere curiosity or not we did not know. We were desperately determined to stick to these creatures until by some means or other we succeeded in persuading them to guide us back to the shore.

Our time was up. We had probably missed our scheduled return. And the vision of Mason's worried and panicky countenance did not help my peace of mind. If we succeeded in getting back to the ship within the next few minutes, he said, there was a chance for us—not much of a chance, but at least something. And failing that—how could we survive a year in this unfriendly fog?

We had been walking under the trees for perhaps a quarter of an hour when we came to the "village." The word is inaccurate, since even from the short glimpse we were permitted it could be readily seen that only the most primitive of habitations were grouped here. An opening carpeted with a curious long and tough kind of grass, in which rude nests had been trampled out. There were no roofs, although occasionally the grass walls seemed to be woven crudely together. It was as if the innate savagery of the beasts would not brook the indignity of socialization without at least the artificial privacy of grass walls.

But we were stopped at the outskirts of the clearing. The warriors confronted us in a determined semi-circle, and we paused to observe our surroundings. Haworth stepped forward a pace and made a sweeping gesture of invitation in the direction from which we had come. The reptile-men eyed us without reply. He repeated his gesture. Then one of the females in the rear began to hop up and down excitedly and make high-pitched squealing noises. Several others around her imitated the example.

Mason and I had our rifles ready in an instant. Haworth looked more worried than ever and turned his pale, care-worn face toward us as if he wished to speak but just then there was a sharp grunt from inside the closed ranks before us. Out stepped our old friend the chief. He walked slowly up to Haworth and placed one hand actually on his breast. Then he gave a gentle push and backed away a step. Why he chose Haworth I cannot say, unless because of the distinction of his flowing beard.

Haworth stood staring at him, thinking hard. Mason and I stepped forward one on each side of him. Things looked dangerous.

"What will we do if they advance on us?"

"If they do that, perhaps we are saved," was Haworth's surprising rejoinder. "Say nothing, but do as I do."

And then advance they did—the whole line slowly moving, with the chief in the center of it. Mason grasped my arm and we three stepped back a pace. The reptiles stepped forward another stride and we kept our distance. Soon we were walking at a normal gait, surrounded on three sides by our unwitting guides. In a surprisingly short time we had reached the edge of the woods, and here the reptiles promptly turned about and started back.

"After them, quick!" said Haworth. And we did.

In a few minutes the reptile-men halted and again faced us—a trifle uneasily this time, I imagined. Again the chief stepped right up to Haworth and gave him another push. Again the tribe slowly advanced and we retreated before it. This time, however, they seemed determined to finish the job. We were evidently unwelcome, although not enemies. Right out past the woods we proceeded—past the clump of three trees and into the pathless sea of mists. In twenty minutes we sighted the shore before us and I half-turned towards our guides, feeling in an indefinite sort of way that we could now dispense with them. But they had other ideas. Right down to the water's edge they drove us and then stood there determined to see us depart.

Mason was already wading out to where our canvas boat still rode at her line—not more than twelve feet out. He reached it waist deep and towed her back to the rocks, climbing out of the water and shaking his legs. Then as Haworth and myself stepped into the frail craft and sat down, he made a gallant bow.

"Thank you! If you only knew how much we wanted to get back here, you would have done this in the first place. Farewell my friends, and don't forget that some day men like us will return to Venus. If they try to buy your village for twenty-four dollars' worth of dinosaur meat, don't be surprised!"

With which reflections he took his place with us in the boat and we pushed off from shore. The reptile-men stood quietly until the mists swallowed us up. I was rowing and the sea was quiet, with slow oily swells lifting us and lowering us regularly. Along the shore we went and then struck out toward the tall shadow we knew was our rocket ship. We had been away more than thirty hours—how much more? Were our watches trustworthy? With all the speed possible to our bodies—weary to our bones and experiencing the inevitable reaction from all our exertion and strain, both physical and mental—we climbed the rungs up the side of the *Asteroid,* leaving the little boat tied at the bottom. Mason burst through the hastily opened air locks and stopped, as though the life had been drained out of him.

The ship's clock read 103—18:36. We were over one hour too late!

Once inside, with the doors shut and the refrigerators on full blast, we stripped off our sodden, grimy clothing; washed ourselves copiously, with reckless disregard now for our water supply; donned dry garments and felt ravenously hungry. I have noticed that many times. Go through a time of danger, even if it be unaccompanied by physical exertion, and the body demands nourishment. In silence we ate, but we made a thorough meal. There was fresh meat miraculously from the refrigerator, crisp biscuits from the sealed tins and a long cool drink of whiskey soda to top it off. Above all, the blessed cool, dry air of the *Asteroid* was delicious to our steamed and soaked bodies. We were hopeless, perhaps, but very comfortable. I don't remember when I fell asleep.

THERE is one peculiar psychological result of travel to other planets, and that is that it gives one an awareness of the exact appearance of the familiar upon returning. I lay in my bunk when I awoke, very pleasantly aware that I was safe for the present and entirely comfortable. My skin was bruised and my muscles were tired, but in a dreamy lethargic fashion not at all unpleasant. The details of the living-cabin were unnaturally clear and sharp to my eyes. That peculiar roundish corner where the pump room floor joined the ship hull, the flattened sides of the little control levers beside me, the garbage door above the stove, with its not quite square outline—everything seemed slightly unfamiliar and made a sharp clean-cut impression on my senses.

This I attribute to the fact that for thirty-odd hours we had seen absolutely nothing that was familiar. Every leaf, every rock, every pool of water must be watched. It might represent some danger or prove a valuable discovery. Our eyes and, in fact, all our senses had been strained to examine everything with the utmost care. Upon returning to the familiar scenes aboard ship this faculty of awareness persisted for a little. Not since my earliest recollections of childhood, when nothing is entirely familiar to one, had I experienced such a sensation. It was altogether agreeable. I seemed to be in a new and fresh existence. It so invigorated me that I could lie still no longer, but arose briskly and wakened my companions noisily.

Mason was on his feet in a jiffy.

"The minute I can get something to eat, I must see if a return course cannot still be figured."

I had forgotten, all this while, our desperate circumstances. Mason's words plunged me into the depths of gloom once more.

"Our return! You will have more than a year to figure that to your heart's content!"

"Perhaps not!"

"What do you mean?"

"There's just a chance we can still make it," (I made an exclamation.) "Just a minute! It's only a chance. The trouble is it will take at least a week to figure out. Oh, why didn't I prepare some figures for alternate return dates? I had long months of leisure and I simply wasted them!"

But his words put new hope in me.

"Do you really think we have a chance to start back in a week?"

Mason, already busy at the stove, grunted out what I took to be "I think so" and went on silently with his preparations for a meal.

Haworth had not yet risen and being questioned described himself as not feeling at all well. I got out a thermometer and stuck it at a rakish angle in his mouth.

"You can stay there for a week," I said, "and recover your strength. It will take Mason that long to figure out whether you can be sick for a whole year more or have to get well suddenly."

Upon removing the thermometer I was alarmed to see that he had a temperature slightly over 100 degrees. His pulse was weak and, generally speaking, I considered his condition rather serious. Mason had by this time prepared boiled eggs and coffee and we tried to get Haworth to eat some, but after one spoonful he refused any more.

Mason and I discussed our situation out of his hearing, in the pump room.

"You nurse him," said he in conclusion, "and I'll chart a new flight curve."

Mason was to be brought his meals and left entirely undisturbed while I was to run the ship. I left him hard at work and descended to sit beside my patient. All that day Haworth lay in his cot. I played cribbage with him and read from the Encyclopedia (how I wished for an amusing story!) and he seemed to be recovering his strength satisfactorily. After fifteen hours Mason descended and we put out the lights in the living-cabin and went to sleep.

Haworth woke us. He was sitting bolt upright when I switched on the lights and reciting poetry in a loud voice, his beard wagging wildly on his chest. Badly mixed and garbled verses he spouted—Shakespeare, Milton and Rudyard Kipling. We would have been amused had it not been so frightening. Hour after hour we worked over him, trying to quiet him. But we had to strap him down to his cot in the end and I gave him a shot of morphine from the medicine cabinet.

We arose after a few hours of broken sleep and Mason resolutely went up above to continue his mathematical labors. I sat beside Haworth and worried desperately. His temperature was 104 degrees. I had no sort of notion what was the matter. Possibly some sort of strange fever he had caught from the Venus jungles—indeed, what might it not have been?

He wakened after a few hours and was quite out of his head. I brewed some strong tea and squeezed lemons into it. This I forced him to sip as often as I could. It would at least allay the fever temporarily. But he grew worse all day and it was again necessary to quiet him with drugs.

"To Heaven," I heard him mutter. "To Heaven in a rocket."

I had no one to turn to in my perplexity. Mason knew absolutely nothing about medicine and the Encyclopedia was not illuminating, although I spent several hours searching through it with the vague notion that it might have somewhere in it the necessary information that would save our friend's life. Yes, by now I was doubtful if he would recover.

When we slept next, I lay tossing in my cot, rising silently every hour or so to creep in the darkness over to his cot and administer some cold tea. I had of course plenty of quinine, but the first dose of this usually sovereign remedy had caused such a violent retching that I did not dare repeat it.

Finally Mason awoke and switched on the lights. This was our "morning" on the spaceship, and this morning was a sad one. Haworth did not waken. He lay breathing softly and with his eyes sunk deep in his pale cheeks. I could scarcely eat and noticed that Mason had some trouble in swallowing his food. We did not exchange a word. There was nothing to say. He slowly climbed up to the room above and drowned his fears in the concentration of his work. I had no such sedative, but sat despondently on my cot thinking soberly over all that had happened in an effort to solve the riddle of this strange illness.

The attack of the insects, naturally, came to my mind. But that had been so many days ago—surely any poison that might have infected their bites would have had an instant effect? Yet I could not with reason blame any other agency. What weird things they had been! "Mosquitoes," Mason had called them. Mosquitoes...what if they were like our earthly insects in this one thing? What if the "poison" they carried was a disease with which they inoculated their victim, like the yellow-fever mosquito?

"Why then," I exclaimed aloud, "I would inoculate him with immune serum from Mason or myself, who recovered!"

AND I was up in an instant and over to the medicine cabinet where I seized an aseptic syringe and, plunging the point carefully into my forearm, drew it half full of blood.

"Come," I thought, "this is not the way to do. There must be no blood in the serum."

Then I paused with the thought that this whole idea was a tissue of imagination without any facts behind it. Should I continue? How should I proceed? I pondered for five minutes and had answered both questions. First I would inoculate Haworth. If the disease had been caused by the huge "insects" or not, there was nevertheless a probability that I had been exposed to the same illness he had, wherever he had got it. Therefore I, being well, might have immune serum in my blood and remote as the chance might be, I had absolutely no other possibility of treatment.

As to the serum, I had an idea. I turned on the stove and placed my left hand, palm up, very firmly upon the hot metal. An instant of pain was sufficient and I promptly treated my new burn with oil and dressed it carefully. In an hour I had an enormous blister on the back of my hand and drew off a full syringe of clear serum. This I injected into my patient's right arm.

All this may sound a trifle heroic, as I write it here. The actual fact was that it hurt very badly for only the first few minutes and during those minutes I wished very strongly that I had not thought of this means of obtaining clear serum. Once done, there was of course nothing heroic about continuing the operation.

I was restless and Haworth remained unconscious. So I climbed up into the pump room and opened the air lock, sitting on the floor of the vestibule with my feet dangling over. After the comfortable coolness of the *Asteroid* the air of Venus hit me like a warm wet sigh. Dim in the surrounding mists I could make out the shore—jungle and mud. Occasionally the visibility would increase as the wind freshened and at such times I could see on the right the line of rocks where we had landed.

I mused upon our exploration of Venus. In all, I thought, we have covered less than one square mile of land. In that "explored" territory we lost ourselves three times. We had observed a few species of reptiles and half a dozen kinds of trees—mainly cycads. Now we are frantically preparing to leave, if we could. I was, perhaps, unjust, since we certainly had traversed some thousands of miles of water and this might be termed exploring the planet in a sense. Certainly we had determined the fact that a large portion of the surface of this planet was liquid.

I gazed down upon this water as I sat there and saw the waves had risen considerably. Our ship was not affected by them, since she was firmly aground on the mud beneath. The breeze seemed to be increasing and as I sat watching a furious gust came along. The mist swirled and thinned out and for two minutes there sprang into view the entire coast before me.

I shouted for Mason and he came instantly to stand beside me in the narrow vestibule. Half a mile away on the low slope of bare rock stood our three tree ferns and back of them the line of forest. The mists cleared still farther and we saw for an instant miles of landscape—great hills rising in the background, dotted with verdure. The light increased more and more. We followed the line of hills up until they lost themselves in the mist, but I distinctly saw a golden glow over them as if the sun had sent its rays through the enveloping atmosphere to point them out to us. It lasted an instant, like a promise, and then the mists closed out the hills and we saw nothing but the miles of rocks and jungle. Then the wind slackened still more and the fog closed down until we could barely make out the nearby shore.

Mason gasped, as though he had been holding his breath throughout the whole revelation.

"That might be a place worth visiting!"

I agreed.

"On the top of those hills the sun might occasionally shine. Not too often, for it would then be intolerably warm, but enough to let a man see where he was going."

"Why would it be so warm?" and then I answered my own question. "Oh, of course, we're thirty million miles nearer the sun than the Earth is."

We sat in thought a moment. Then I told him my fears for Haworth and the means I had taken.

"If he shows no improvement in another hour," I added, "I am going to inject your serum. Whatever disease he may have, it might have passed me by and touched you."

"Suppose he was the only one to be favored?"

"If it affected him alone, then I don't think...I'm afraid..."

I left my sentence unfinished for the moment. Mason frowned terrifically and passed his hand over his forehead. We went inside and closed the doors, for it had already become uncomfortably warm inside of the ship. We turned on the refrigerators and soon were quite cool again. He sat down once more to his work and I descended to the living-cabin.

Haworth was still unconscious and seemed weaker—too weak. His pulse was barely detectable. In desperation I filled a glass of whiskey and poured it between his lips. In a few minutes his pulse was stronger and then, suddenly, the sweat came.

I knew what that meant. The fever had broken!

I wrapped him in blankets and strapped them over his body and called up the good news to Mason, whose face promptly appeared in the hole in the ceiling. He was smiling broadly once again.

CHAPTER ELEVEN
Back to Earth

THERE is no need of detailing the steps to recovery. Haworth was ravenously hungry when he woke and I found my job of cook to the ship no sinecure, what with my burned hand. Mason left his figures long enough for one game of cribbage with our patient and spent the rest of his time up above in a very fury of calculation.

"How are you making out?"

"You know, we have a chance—just a chance."

Eight earthly days passed with the same report. Haworth was steadily improving all the time and was more or less up and around when we heard a shout from above. Mason climbed down and joined us in high spirits.

"We start home," he said, studying the clock, which read 112—6:13, "in three hours and twenty-four minutes!"

I uttered a shout of relief and joy.

"But how can we manage to connect with the Earth this late?" objected Haworth. "Venus travels so much faster than the Earth, that we must be past its place in its orbit by now."

"We are," retorted the mathematician, "but only just past it. We have to lose an excess speed of about ten miles a second, in order to land on the earth. Our fifty percent reserve of fuel will do this nicely. We calculated on seven miles a second, you know."

"But if we plan to use all our reserves, aren't we taking a considerable chance?"

Mason shrugged his shoulders.

"Let's be glad we have a chance to take. Would you prefer staying here a year?"

"God forbid!"

Haworth was almost recovered by then. The past few days had done wonders for him. He declared himself ready to take command of the *Asteroid* on her return voyage and with the words scarcely out of his mouth he was clambering up to the pump room, where he spent the next three hours scrambling about the machinery—testing and checking. Everything was exactly as it had been, but that was his way— and not a bad way at that, perhaps. It seemed so good to us to have him up and about, that he might have had I know not how many unusual habits, they would have all appeared sensible and desirable. I mention this, because usually it irritates me to see someone take unnecessary precautions, and to check and recheck the already correct.

We spent a final five minutes at the vestibule door, looking our last on the face of Venus. I do not know exactly what we had expected from our trip. Visions of miraculous discoveries, smiling fertile landscapes, perhaps gold and other precious metals lying about in abundance. But certainly we had none of us expected just what we had found.

As Mason put it: "We could have filled Madison Square Garden with live steam and sat in it for three weeks to about the same advantage! Not only that, but we would have known where we were all the time, in that case!"

But in spite of disappointments, there was a feeling of accomplishment that we all shared. There were few thrilling discoveries, it is true, but just the same we were the first of the human race to visit a planet other than our own. Some day these vague inhospitable shores would be made habitable. This spot where our ship lay grounded in the shallows would be historic. I had my camera with me at the doorway and made a photograph, a print of which is before me now. Dark water and darker jungle and the white fog over all.

We closed the doors and screwed them fast and made our way to the cots.

"Ready?" called Haworth, his hand on the starting lever.

Mason and I turned to our duties and felt the ship lurch as the power was applied. We were pressed deeply into our cots and our bodies were heavy under the steady acceleration. The dials moved slowly and the misty surface of the periscope glass grew brighter each moment.

Suddenly the mist vanished and bright sunlight almost blinded us.

Mason twisted the controls until we had located our objective, a small star in a peculiar triangle formation, and then Haworth made a warning sign to us and turned on the power to full acceleration. Now we felt the pressure severely. I could hardly move my arm to the controls and, lying on my back as I was, it was exceeding difficult to raise my head. There was, however, very little to be done so far as I was concerned. My two companions had most of the control mechanism in their charge and seemed to manage well enough, although they perspired visibly with their efforts.

It lasted only ten minutes or so. The noise of the rocket exhaust had increased to a deafening roar when the last section had been dropped off and the sudden silence came like a blow. Haworth was not quite quick enough in starting up the gyroscope and I was overcome with nausea as my body was suddenly left weightless.

When I had in a measure recovered, Mason was standing over me with raised eyebrows.

"This time you can clean it up yourself. Do you good!"

I complied weakly, and really felt better for the exertion.

The floor was now our partition wall, for the rotation of the ship about her line of flight had again set up an artificial gravity outwards in all directions. I observed that the speed indicator and other instruments no longer registered, for we were entirely out of the atmosphere of Venus. We were coasting freely at almost ten miles a second back to Earth! How eagerly we looked in the periscope glass as Mason brought into view our home planet! There it stood, a pure white ball of minute proportions, although larger than any of the stars that glowed so much more violently around it. Then he turned the ship until Venus swung into line and we saw the huge surface we were leaving, all glistening on one half where the sun struck it slantingly and a dirty gray-black on the shadowed portion. But white or gray, it was all the same blinding mist—the curse of the planet.

And now if I am to be kind to my readers I will spare them the details of the next ninety days. After our hardships upon Venus we were mentally and bodily exhausted and quite content for some weeks to rest in complete sloth. Then we felt the need of amusement and occupation and I, for one, passed the time very pleasantly by working my observations and specimens into the form of notes. Then I had a number of photographs to develop and print and additional astronomical pictures to take. I did not hurry my tasks and interspersed my working hours liberally with less serious occupations. Our cribbage tournament was revived and we even became interested in three-handed auction bridge for a while. Mason and Haworth were equally well occupied. We knew what to expect and were not too impatient. But hardly a single detail of this period stands out clearly in my memory.

Venus and all we had seen there had become a dream. It was difficult to believe that we had really been there. We seemed to have been living forever in this space ship, adrift in the abyss.

IT came as a distinct shock when Mason announced from the periscope that the Earth was growing visibly larger. But a glance at the ship's clock showed 189—2:57. We were due to land in less than two weeks! We clustered about the glass, observing with delight our native world. She showed about three inches across, like a tiny moon. And in fact her own moon was now distinctly visible, a gleaming disk three-quarters of an inch in diameter. And of exceeding interest to Mason this moon was, since the hidden side was exposed to our view and brightly lighted.

"It must be a new moon on Earth," said Mason and no remark he could have made would have brought to me more clearly the fact that we were wanderers in strange places.

We had the leisure to make a thorough observation of the hidden side of the Earth's satellite during the next week and Mason was vastly busy making notes, while I took photographs at his direction. Full details of his findings are of course available to the interested reader in his recently published monograph on the subject. And as all the world knows by now, nothing essentially different exists on that side than on the other. On the voyage out, we had been able to see a small sector of this unknown portion, but not until now had we such leisure and opportunity to make a detailed observation.

As the days passed the Earth took on additional form and detail. It was a glorious sight to our eyes! And a last look in the other direction showed a tiny dot of soft white light—all that could be seen of Venus. Soon I thought, we shall gaze on her from the Earth and see not the familiar evening star, but the cold unwinking eye of a reptile-man, or the baleful orb of *Dinosaur Tyrannus Rex!*

But Haworth was busy preparing for our landing man-euvers, and I was sufficiently familiar with these by now to take an intelligent interest. When we had shut off our motors after leaving Venus we had exhausted the fuel of the second step of the *Asteroid* and discarded it, continuing our flight in the small eighty-ton third step formerly contained in its nose. It was in this small ship, of course, that the controls and cabins were centered. The fuel of this ship, in turn, had been almost entirely exhausted so that it was necessary, as Haworth pointed out, to make a perfect landing.

"For if we don't," he said, "we have no power left to rectify an imperfect one."

He had already turned the handle and set the pumps to work projecting our wings. This required practically no effort while we were still in space. It could have been done by hand, had that been necessary.

"I believe," he said, "we will endeavor to commence our landing circles at the equator. Then as we slacken speed we can verge northward, consequently shortening our circles. We will have to land where we can, of course, for we have no power to waste choosing a suitable spot."

I suggested that we would need to land in water and for that reason might do best to land near the equator line, for in this zone much more water occurs than land.

"And," I continued, "if any change be made from the equatorial circle, why not southward, for a less proportion of land exists in the Southern Hemisphere than in the Northern?"

Haworth agreed with me, after a moment's thought.

"However," he added, "I believe we can find either the Atlantic or the Pacific Ocean easily enough and on the other hand, have you ever thought what might happen if we landed in the South Atlantic, thousands of miles from the ocean traffic lanes? One can be very thoroughly lost even on our own familiar Earth, you know."

This was true, of course, but I confess that any part of the Earth whatsoever had seemed safe haven a moment before he spoke.

"The Northern Hemisphere, in the Temperate Zone, is much the most civilized portion of the globe. As to a landing place, we might even be lucky enough to reach Long Island Sound—or perhaps even our little lake in Connecticut. And the Great Lakes have distinct possibilities, as well."

It may sound strange to hear a planet some eight thousand miles in diameter discussed in this fashion. But following this conversation I went to the periscope glass and gazed for many painstaking minutes before I could be sure I recognized the dark line that was the Mediterranean Sea!

Our landing maneuvers were to be the same as before. We entered the atmosphere at a high altitude (about seventy miles) and the air was so rare at this height that even our speed of almost five miles a second did not cause sufficient friction to endanger our ship. Our wings turned in a small arc, so that at first they were used to hold the *Asteroid* down towards the Earth, for our terrific speed tended to make us flyaway again into space. But we used the wings to force us around the globe again and again in a circle.

We circumnavigated the world in less than an hour and a half at first. Then the friction slowly lessened our speed and permitted gravity to affect our course downward. Then the wings were inclined the other way, so as to support us in the air. As our speed lessened we descended still lower, until at last we were traveling at about two or three hundred miles an hour and ready for a landing, similar to that of a fast airplane. At such a speed a landing was difficult, but if made in smooth water our staunch metal hull would protect us from damage.

The whole maneuver went through exactly as planned. Haworth and Mason were at the controls as before, and the operation required some seventeen hours to perform. We entered the atmosphere of Earth at 202—0:14 by the ship's dock.

I could observe the periscope glass from my cot, except for occasional moments when Mason's head was in the way. The Earth had long since loomed up until it filled half the entire sky and as we entered the atmosphere I could see oceans and continents sweep by beneath us like a panorama designed by a madman. The strain and worry was visible on Mason's frowning face and Haworth clawed nervously at his black beard half the time. I myself was without special duty for the most part, although for a five-hour stretch I relieved Mason at the periscope.

"If we could only make a landing somewhere near the United States," Haworth was repeating over and over to himself.

Mason laughed.

"It would be a fine thing if we ended up shipwrecked in the middle of the ocean! Do try and land in New York harbor, old man! Near Quarantine, if you can, for I understand they are most particular down there about vessels arriving from foreign ports!"

For the last two minutes I relinquished the periscope controls to Mason. We were over Spain at the time and traveling west at less than two miles a second. Haworth was jubilant.

"We'll just about make it," he prophesied.

And we did. We had been scudding over the Atlantic for an hour and a half, at constantly lessening speed, when I noticed that the surface of the water showing in the glass had become more detailed. Instead of a smooth sheet of lead-colored matter, separate ripples were now discernible. Then the ripples grew into small wave lines and these enlarged until the familiar seascape spread before us not a mile below.

"Hold fast!" warned Haworth.

We all made sure of our fastenings and positions.

Suddenly the waves loomed up swift and huge in the glass and a great white splash wiped out all vision. At the same time the *Asteroid* gave a terrific lurch and rolled over and over several times. Then all was still once more, except for a strong steady heave of the vessel in the trough of the seas. Our cabin was now as it had been several times before. Our floors had turned into the circular hull wall, for the ship floated upright. None of us had been hurt in the slightest, but the cabin was a chaos, for the kitchen cabinet had burst open and the Encyclopedia Britannica was indiscriminately mingled with pots and pans and a thoughtlessly open can of photograph-developing fluid!

The ship's clock read 202—17:02. The voyage was over.

We climbed, the three of us, up the rungs on the water tank, through the opening in what was now our ceiling, and into the pump room, now above us. Mason wrenched at the lever and flung open the vestibule door. I darted into the vestibule and opened the air lock door to the outside world. The ocean breeze was full in our faces and filled the cabin with a delicious odor. It was unbelievably invigorating after six months in artificial atmosphere, and three weeks of Venus' steamy air, impregnated with chlorine. We crowded in the tiny entrance, arms about each other's shoulders, and breathed it in as if we could never have enough.

THE rest is history. Everyone within reach of a radio or newspaper knows that Captain Turnbull of the British tramp steamer *Gardenia* picked us up a hundred miles east of the Long Island coast. Haworth offered him enormous largesse if he would tow the *Asteroid* into New York and we even lived aboard our own little vessel during the twenty-four hours this required, (the wind was quartering against him). The captain, good man, left the management of his own ship to his first mate when he found out what was afoot, for he was aboard our vessel most of the short trip, staring open-mouthed at one or the other of us, listening and asking questions.

The *Gardenia* had a radio on board and it had been in frantic use, evidently, for when we reached New York harbor the official city tug met us and we were constrained to leave the *Asteroid* in charge of Captain Turnbull and be officially welcomed by the City of New York. Haworth arranged that our rocket ship would be anchored in an inaccessible section of the harbor and well guarded and that we would come back for her later on. Then we went with the officials.

Many of you who read this may have seen us riding through bedlam in an automobile that day and wondered what we were thinking about. For myself, I was thinking how happy I was and how glad and good it felt to see a million or so human beings once again—particularly since they seemed glad to see me! We couldn't have had too much fuss and noise to suit my taste just then—although I will admit there is a limit to all pleasures, as we have since found out.

One more scene and I am done. A few nights ago, Dr. Mason and myself dined at the Charles Bascomb Haworth mansion in Connecticut at Mr. Haworth's special invitation.

"Bigelow," he said, "your moving picture films and photographs have been sold on a royalty basis to a well-known syndicate."

I nodded.

"Do you know what the royalties have amounted to in the single month that has elapsed since our return? Over two and a half million dollars!"

I suppressed an exclamation and Mason looked up with raised eyebrows.

"I have estimated the entire cost of the *Asteroid,* including all test flights, and find it amounts to very little more than that sum," continued Haworth. "It is certain that in a few months more, what with further royalties on the pictures and the income from your book and Mason's scientific writings, we will have a substantial income above all costs of the expedition. This, naturally, we share equally."

So the voyage to Venus, barren of treasure as it seemed at first, has finally resulted in modest wealth for us all. I have bought over the ownership of *Lens and Bellows* and find I have made a very comfortable investment. Mason and I still live together, though he talks of starting off for the Mount Wilson Observatory next month to spend at least a part of his sabbatical year as originally intended!

Haworth, as the world knows, has buried himself in his Connecticut estate. What is not generally known is that he is working. He says he has an idea and Mason and I find it uninteresting to visit him, for his time is spent entirely in his study where he sits brooding over books, stroking his beard the while, or pacing the floor in deep concentration. As Mason says, "Of course we are welcome to go for walks with him—the length of the study and back! But I'm tired of being confined to rooms."

With the enormous mass of public interest directed upon the subject, it is not surprising that as I write no less than three space ships are building. Both the ships of the German Interplanetary Society and the French Air Corps are designed for voyages to the moon's frozen surface. The American Interplanetary Society (their membership jumped to 50,000 last week, I am told) plan a vessel to visit either Mars, or Venus for a more satisfactory exploration. All three of us have been invited to take places—in fact to assume leadership—in this expedition.

It would be idle to say that I am content to remain in comfort here forever. It is good to be back, of course, but there is something very irritating to me about the half-finished nature of our exploration on Venus. With fog-piercing searchlights a very great deal may be possible on that planet. The General Magnetic Company has been good enough to turn their laboratories to work on this problem. If they succeed and if a ship is available—well, I won't say what might eventually happen. But that lies in the bosom of the future.

THE END

REVOLT WAS BREWING IN THE FAR-OFF PLANETS

Alan Tremaine was the son of Richard Tremaine, one of the most respected leaders in the Outworlds. But when an assassin cut down the elder statesman, the younger Tremaine found the leadership of the Outworlds suddenly thrust into his lap. But there was something amiss, and when violence and revolt suddenly flared, Termaine found himself torn between the loyalty he had for his father's visions of the future, and his own personal ideals. But there was a traitor afoot—with a daring plan of destruction and conquest.

Tremaine knew Mars received its water via the massive space warp that ran between Mars and Venus. And he knew that if someone cut this interplanetary lifeline it meant war—and possibly the destruction of mankind…

CAST OF CHARACTERS

ALAN TREMAINE
It's tough being the son of a legendary political figure, especially when you're expected to lead the planets into interplanetary war.

BENNETT KEIFER
He was the steadfast advisor to one of the most powerful men in the Solar System, but could he really be trusted?

LAURA OLMSTEAD
She'd met Alan Tremaine on a space voyage to Mars and was smitten with him, but her affections would soon be put to the test.

CAPTAIN HADDIX
He aligned himself with the forces of total conquest—and you never wanted want to turn your back on him.

GENERAL OLMSTEAD
This Earth general was loyal and dedicated, but he wasn't crazy about putting the Outworlds on equal footing with Earth.

PRESIDENT HOLLAND
He was faced with something that no U.S. President had ever faced before—the imminent destruction of Earth.

BILL GRAHAM
All he was asked to do was to watch over a good-looking dame for a few hours—but it got him a lot more than he bargained for.

REVOLT OF THE OUTWORLDS

By
MILTON LESSER

ARMCHAIR FICTION
PO Box 4369, Medford, Oregon 97504

*For more information about Armchair Books and products, visit our
website at…*

www.armchairfiction.com

Or email us at…

armchairfiction@yahoo.com

CHAPTER ONE

AMPLIFIERS swelled the clarion call of the trumpet above the keening Martian wind that swept into the great central plaza of Syrtis Major City. Two hundred thousand Outworld citizens, the entire population of Syrtis, huddled together in the cold and watched the blue and gold banner of the Outworld Federation run up the pole to flutter proudly beside the globe-and-stars flag of Earth.

There was a tremendous roar from the crowd as Alan Tremaine climbed the long flight of steps leading to the platform in the center of the plaza. *It's really my father they're applauding,* Alan Tremaine thought. The elder Tremaine, dead these two weeks, had made the dream of independence a reality for the Outworlds. Then, on the eve of success, he had been struck down by a still unknown assassin. Alan had been rushed from New Washington University on Earth by the Outworld Federation, to bring the magic name of Tremaine to the ceremony on Mars.

Above him now, Alan could see the military governor of Mars, Lieutenant General Roderick Olmstead, waiting alongside the banks of huge television screens, which showed similar scenes on Venus, on Saturn's great moon Titan, and on the four large Jovian satellites. But the eyes of all the Outworlds were here on Mars as Alan Tremaine mounted the platform to accept the Declaration of Sovereignty from the governor.

A hush descended on the crowd as General Olmstead unrolled the scroll and held it before the television cameras. "On behalf of the government of Earth," he said, his voice booming across the Syrtis plaza on the amplifiers, "I present this Declaration of Sovereignty to the people of all the Outworlds. The five hundred million citizens of Mars, Venus, Titan and the Jovian Moons will hereafter march alongside the peoples of Earth in Equal Union."

Two hundred thousand voices rose in a thunderous peal of acclaim.

"It is to your everlasting credit," General Olmstead went on, "that your great struggle for freedom bears fruit today bloodlessly. History shall long remember this moment, for the grim alternative of war was always present but shunned by your very great leader, Richard Tremaine."

There was not a sound now in all the vast crowd. Alan Tremaine thought it must be the same elsewhere, with half a billion Outworld citizens watching on their television screens across the solar system.

"The one tragedy of your greatest moment," General Olmstead concluded, "is that Richard Tremaine did not live to see it become a reality. I now place this scroll in the hands of his only son, Alan Tremaine."

His eyes suddenly misty, Alan accepted the Declaration of Sovereignty from General Olmstead. The long political struggle, climaxed today on the windswept plaza of Syrtis Major City, was not his. Attending New Washington University on Earth, he had missed the dramatic sequence of events that led to this day. Almost, he felt like an outsider. But he believed in their fight even if he had had no active part in it. And the name Tremaine was now lifted into the pale sky above Syrtis Plaza on two hundred thousand voices.

"Tremaine! Tremaine! Speech! Speech!"

Alan took a deep breath and cleared his throat. Faces as numerous as the desert sands of Mars gazed up at him. Untold millions more watched their television screens on the other Outworlds. Seated beside her father, Laura Olmstead smiled at him.

"I humbly accept this Declaration of Sovereignty on behalf of all the Outworlds and on behalf of my father," Alan said. "I'm sure that on this day my father would offer thanks to God that our freedom was achieved without violence."

JUST then the television screens depicting smaller ceremonies on the other Outworlds erupted into violent activity. There was muted thunder from the Venus screen. People could be seen running about wildly, the drone of jets was heard. Brilliant light flared, blanking the screen momentarily. When it could be seen again, a mushroom-topped atomic cloud was rising from the crater that had been the Governor's Headquarters on Venus. The scene was the same on Titan and the four Jovian Moons.

A voice blared: "Attention! Attention Mars. This is Government Station, Ganymede. Seconds ago, the Outworld Federation met freedom with treachery. Even as tactical atomic weapons were used on the Government Headquarters, their speakers were proclaiming peaceful union. But now the masses have risen behind the spectre of military violence. 'Equal Union is not enough,' their leaders cry. 'We're ready to fight for total independence!' The traitorous Federation militia is marching on the underground Government Station here. Protect yourself, Mars!" Abruptly, the staccato blast of an automatic hand weapon could be heard. The voice from Ganymede was stilled.

General Olmstead rushed to the microphone, pushing Alan roughly aside. "All Martian units!" he cried. "Prepare for war. Directive A-2, this headquarters, put into immediate effect. Martial law is proclaimed. All civilian authority is hereby terminated. Protect the space field and the government station. All commissioned leaders of the

Outworld Federation on Mars will surrender themselves, weaponless, to the military authorities. Those who resist face immediate arrest." All at once, the microphone squawked into silence. Someone had cut off the generators below the platform.

"Tremaine," General Olmstead raged, "your father is better off dead. Seeing this happen would have killed him. Your name will go down in history, all right—as the worst traitor since Benedict Arnold."

Alan shook his head. It all had happened so fast, his senses were still numb with shock. The Federation had told him nothing about this. The Federation had been content with Equal Union, his father's dream. True, a militant minority group within the Federation had longed for total independence, through violence if necessary, but Richard Tremaine had always opposed this. Now, it had happened.

Military control of Venus, Titan and the Jovian moons was inadequate. In hours, the governments would fall. The same was true for the smaller centers of Martian population, but Earth maintained its strongest military garrison in Syrtis Major City. Here the Earth forces, under General Olmstead, could probably hold their own.

But it was open revolt now, something that the dead Richard Tremaine had opposed as steadfastly as he had opposed Earth domination of the Outworlds.

"I didn't know," Alan began. "Nobody told me..."

His voice was drowned in a swirling sea of sound as Federation militiamen threw their wind cloaks and revealed the uniforms beneath them as they charged up the steps toward the platform. Government soldiers, storming up the other side, waited for them. As yet, not a weapon had been fired in Syrtis.

"Stop!" Alan cried, rushing to the edge of the platform. "Are you insane? We wanted Equal Union. We've been granted Equal Union. Put down your weapons and go home."

THE front rank of the militiamen, three abreast on the stairs, paused. This was a Tremaine talking. There was a difference between father and son, of course, but a Tremaine had made this day possible.

The leader of the militiamen, a bearded fellow in the uniform of a major, shook his head. "You don't know Mr. Tremaine. You weren't here when your father spoke his last words. We're carrying out the orders of Richard Tremaine!"

Two government soldiers who had mounted the other side of the platform came up behind Alan and pinned his arms to his sides. "Go ahead and fire," one of them said. "Kill Tremaine's son, why don't you?"

The front rank of militiamen was being pressed up the stairs from behind, but had returned their weapons to their sides. Alan struggled with the soldiers who held him. Below the platform, the vast crowd was seething restlessly, watching the drama unfold above them. The thin sprinkling of government soldiers in their midst could be swept under in seconds unless government station reinforcements were sent at once.

Alan thrust his elbow back, felt it jar against the ribs of one of the soldiers. The man gasped as the air was forced from his lungs. Still gasping, he was spun around by Alan and hurled down on the militiamen mounting the stairs at the head of the platform. Alan whirled, but the second soldier was on him, circling his neck with a powerful arm. They went down together, thrashing and rolling across the platform.

Something roared overhead. Alan was aware of General Olmstead, his daughter Laura huddled behind him, pointing up at the sky. Then a shadow passed swiftly over the platform, came back—and hovered. The roar was replaced by a loud clattering. Still wrestling with the soldier, Alan could see a jet-copter, switching from jets to rotors, hanging half a dozen feet above the platform like an enormous black grasshopper.

More militiamen leaped from the copter to join those swarming up the stairs, their hand weapons spitting death at the first rank of government soldiers that had come up the other side of the platform. The revolution in Syrtis Major City was an actual fact now.

"Get down!" General Olmstead told his daughter. "Flatten yourself."

But the brief firing atop the platform had cleared it of government soldiers. Rope ladders were dropped from the jet-copter.

"Tremaine," someone called from above. "Climb up quickly."

To remain here in Syrtis Major City was madness. Alan could accomplish nothing in the chaos of revolt. Besides, the militiaman had said this was his father's final wish. Armed rebellion for total independence. He had to find out. He caught the swaying rope ladder in his hands and mounted it. At the same moment, General Olmstead and his daughter were forced up another rope ladder at atomic pistol point.

Its passengers securely inside, the jet-copter rose a hundred feet above the platform on its flashing, clattering rotors. Then the jets were cut in and the craft streaked north from Syrtis Major City at supersonic speed.

CHAPTER TWO

"LIES," General Olmstead said bitterly. "Don't tell me anything. It's all lies."

"I swear I knew nothing about this," Alan insisted.

"Do you realize what you've done? Thousands of innocent people must have died already in the atomic explosions on the Outworlds. Millions more will perish before this war comes to an end. For it's war you've brought to the solar system, Alan Tremaine. Is that what your father would have wanted?"

"I brought nothing," Alan said. "I don't know what my father would have wanted."

"I believe him, Dad," Laura Olmstead said. Alan had met her for the first time two weeks ago on the spaceship from Earth. She was going to join her father on Mars for the Declaration of Sovereignty ceremony. Alan had struck up a quick friendship with her in his darkest moments—when the death of his father had seemed so tragic, bringing Alan's world tumbling down about him. Laura Olmstead's understanding, her frank sympathy, then her cheerful talk and companionship as the two-week space journey wore on, had done much to help Alan. They had parted at the Syrtis Major spaceport, to meet again three days later as revolution unexpectedly engulfed Mars and the other Outworlds.

"Alan Tremaine is a traitor to Earth and his own people as well," General Olmstead told his daughter now. "I won't hear anything more about it."

Half a dozen militiamen sat about the cabin of the jet-copter with them. Up front, a pilot and a co-pilot were at the controls.

"Alan's new on Mars, Dad. He's been at school on Earth, remember that," Laura said in a near whisper.

The leader of the militiamen turned to Alan and said, "We're approaching Red Sands now, sir. Do you wish to go right down or look over the fortifications from the air?"

"Red Sands?" Alan asked. "What's that?"

"Operation Headquarters, sir. Your lieutenants are waiting for you to take charge of the revolution, sir."

"So he's new on Mars," General Olmstead told his daughter. "So he doesn't know a thing about this. He's running the whole show, Laura. He's got us for hostages, too, or didn't you realize it? Earth will think twice about attacking Federation Headquarters with us prisoner there."

Alan was going to tell General Olmstead and his daughter they wouldn't remain hostages long if he could help it, but the militiaman was waiting for his answer. He said, "Let's go right down. Who's in charge of the Headquarters, soldier?"

"Why, you are, sir."

"No. I mean right now."

"Bennett Keifer, sir. Your father's right-hand man."

"Let's go down and meet this Bennett Keifer," Alan said. And, to Laura: "Don't worry about anything, Laura. It's going to be all right."

But when he reached for her hand, she withdrew it and would not meet his eyes directly.

THERE was nothing but the ochre wastelands of Mars, the dunes marching, windswept, from horizon to horizon. Far away to the east, a thin green line knifed across the rusty sands where vegetation clung precariously to the banks of a

Martian canal, nurtured by the waters it brought down from the melting polar cap.

The militiamen flanked them on either side as they walked across the desert, two uniformed figures remaining behind long enough to cover the jet-copter with an ochre-colored tarpaulin, which would effectively camouflage it from the air. It was like something from the Arabian Nights, Alan thought as they approached a low, rocky escarpment thrusting up through the sand. The leader of the militiamen placed his hand against a polished spot on the surface of the rock, which pulsed with the contact as a hidden device checked the pattern and whorls of the militiaman's fingerprints. The effect was the same as the *Open Sesame* of the Arabian Nights, for a great slab-like section of the escarpment rolled ponderously aside, revealing a dark cavity.

"Red Sands," the militiaman said proudly, and led the way inside.

Alan was totally unprepared for what happened next. The door in the rock rolled shut behind them. Lights blazed inside the cavern, brighter than the pale Martian day. A throbbing, busy city was spread out before them below the surface of Mars.

Throngs of men, women and children lined the short road to the city on both sides. A great cry went up from them as Alan, the militiamen, General Olmstead and his daughter approached.

"Hail, Tremaine!" The cry echoed from the rock walls of the underground city. "Hail, Tremaine!" It rolled from the far throbbing reaches of the bustling city. "Tremaine, Tremaine, Tremaine!"

Not for me, Alan thought. *For my father.* What, actually did he know about all this? Perhaps a revolution directed from the secret base here at Red Sands had been his father's secret dream. The adulation with which the people of Red Sands greeted him filled him with a sense of pride. Not for his own accomplishments, but for his father's. Laura Olmstead was, quite suddenly and unexpectedly, part of a different world. Alan shrugged, deciding to suspend judgment until he met and talked with Bennett Keifer.

Now there were cries of: "He looks like his father!" "See, the same brow, the same bearing!" "The eyes are the same, I tell you. We have Richard Tremaine with us all over again!" And always, from all sides: "Hail, Tremaine!"

Alan caught Laura's gaze and tried to smile at her. She was on the verge of tears. "The sycophantic hypocrites," she said. "It's disgusting, carrying on like this while people are dying all over the solar system."

"It isn't for me," Alan told her desperately. "It's in memory of my father."

Laura's eyelids squeezed shut. Tears on her cheeks, she walked blindly ahead, supported by her father's arm. "I hate you, Alan Tremaine," she said.

"TREMAINE," Bennett Keifer said half an hour later, shaking his hand with vigorous enthusiasm. "You look so much like your father I could have picked you out of any crowd. Sit down, boy."

Alan shook his head. "Thanks, but I'll stand." General Olmstead and his daughter had been left off elsewhere while Alan had been ushered into the Administration Center of Red Sands, a great rectangular structure carved from the subterranean rock of Mars. Finally, he had stood face to face with Bennett Keifer. A big, handsome man in the uniform of a Federation colonel, Keifer had flashing eyes and a direct manner that Alan found disarming.

"I'm sure you have many questions," Keifer said.

"Just one. Did my father sanction this armed revolt?"

"What a strange question. Of course he did."

"Nobody told me before."

"We couldn't reveal it today, Tremaine. Not even to you. We couldn't chance revealing it until our forces had moved on all the Outworlds."

"In his letters, my father always said the glorious thing about the Outworld Federation was how it had achieved its ends bloodlessly."

"Tremaine, I'm telling you, I was here. They brought your father here after he was shot. He died with me at his side. He died saying that the Earth government was trying to trick us. Equal Union was a farce, he said. Equal Union—with Earth bleeding the Outworlds dry of their resources! Don't you see, Tremaine? Earth needs our mineral wealth—heavy water from Venus, iron from Mars, lithium and cobalt from the Jovian moons and Titan. They'll bleed us dry and pay next to nothing for our mineral wealth. Since theirs is the only market, we have no choice. The only alternative was armed revolt for the full freedom Earth wouldn't grant us."

"But in Equal Union we had an equal, representative vote for the first time. This Earth granted us."

"Representative vote, Tremaine. There's the catch. There are ten people on Earth for every Outworlder. What kind of equality is that?"

"I don't know," Alan admitted. I think my father would have—"

"I'm telling you what your father said. I was there. Why don't you do this, Tremaine: get acquainted with our city. I don't want to rush you. When you're ready to take over and make the decisions, I'll step aside. How does that sound?"

"I don't want to usurp your authority just because my name's Tremaine," Alan said. "I don't understand this, not yet. I'm going to try, though." He was suddenly weary. It was the same feeling he had when news of his father's death had reached him on Earth. The world tumbling down about his shoulders. Atlas trying to hold up the globe but shorn of all his strength.

He said, "Is there someplace I can go to clean up? My head feels like it's spinning."

"Someplace to go," Keifer repeated the words, smiling. "Your father's apartment here in Red Sands is yours. I'll have one of our enlisted men show you the way. And take your time about things, Tremaine. No one is rushing you."

Alan thanked him and said, "What about General Olmstead and his daughter?"

"Don't you worry. Naturally, they're prisoners of war. But they'll be well cared for here. We're civilized people, Tremaine."

THEY shook hands again, then Alan followed a militiaman outside through the corridors of Red Sands to a large apartment quarried in the rock wall of the underground city. He dismissed the enlisted man and found a bent elderly figure waiting for him inside.

The man had gray hair and thin, stooped shoulders—as if he had spent the better part of his life pouring over books. He spoke in a thin, reedy voice, choked with emotion, "Is anyone waiting for you outside?" he inquired.

Alan shook his head.

"Then listen to me. I shouldn't be here. If Keifer knew…" The elderly man shrugged. "…I don't know what might happen. Alan, I am Eugene Talbrick. Does the name mean anything to you?"

"Yes, Alan nodded. "My father wrote about you often. He said you were always a pillar of strength to him, a…"

"No matter," said Talbrick. You have heard of me. Alan, the good name of Tremaine is being used to bathe the solar system in blood!"

"What are you talking about?"

"Keifer. He says your father secretly wanted armed revolt. It's not true, Alan. And do you realize what Keifer plans to make of you?"

Alan frowned. Eugene Talbrick, his father had always written, was an inspirational figure behind everything the Outworld Federation stood for. If Richard Tremaine had been the eloquent spokesman for freedom, Talbrick was the thinker. If Tremaine could be compared to Washington historically then surely Talbrick could be compared to an older Thomas Jefferson, or Ben Franklin perhaps. "No," Alan said. "I've only just met Keifer."

"You'll be a figurehead, Alan. Listen."

Talbrick walked to a television screen on the wall and soon had it working. A grave-faced news commentator was saying, "...nuts all over Syrtis Major City. The magic name of Tremaine is on everyone's lips. Richard the father, Alan the son. If Richard Tremaine had not sanctioned this revolution, the people say, their forces never would have struck all over the solar system. If Alan Tremaine was not here to lead them they might have accepted the Declaration of Sovereignty. But with the memory of one Tremaine and the leadership of another, they will fight now for total freedom.

"Elsewhere on the revolution front, search jets are sweeping wide over the Martian desert for some trace of Governor General Olmstead, who was kidnapped by Federation forces along with his daughter. Up to this moment, no trace of them has been found...

"Here's a bulletin from Earth. Government warships have been dispatched to Venus, Titan and the Jovian Moons to put down the provisional Federation governments that have risen there. Heavy casualties on both sides are feared."

Talbrick blanked the television screen. "Believe me, Alan," he said. "Civilization may depend on your decision.

Your father never sanctioned this armed uprising. Keifer lied. Keifer dreams of an independent Federation that can drive Earth to its knees economically. Or worse. You're to be in command, but he'll pull the strings behind you."

Alan paced back and forth without speaking. He hardly could believe Talbrick any more than he could believe Keifer. The one had been behind his father, offering strength from deep, philosophical wisdom. The other had been beside Richard Tremaine in all his stormy political fights.

Alan smiled without humor. "Charge and counter charge," he said. "My ears will probably be ringing with them. Do you have any proof?"

"Yes," said Eugene Talbrick. "A letter from your father to you. It's in my own quarters now. I wouldn't mail it for fear it would be intercepted on its way to Earth."

"A letter?"

"He knew it was the end. He knew he was dying. He wrote the letter and gave it to me because he had seen through Keifer too late. Will you come with me now?"

"Of course," Alan said, and followed the old man from his father's apartment.

"HERE we are," Eugene Talbrick told him a few minutes later. He opened the door to his own quarters and stepped inside. Alan followed him into darkness, heard the old man groping ahead of him for the switch which would fill the windowless, rock-hewn apartment with light.

The door clicked shut behind them.

"That's funny," Talbrick's reedy voice was close at hand. "The light doesn't work."

There was a soft series of repeated thuds, someone moving across the carpet quickly.

"Who's there?" Eugene Talbrick caned.

"Look out!" Alan cried, suddenly wary. He brushed past the old man and collided with someone there in the darkness. Briefly they struggled, then something struck the side of Alan's head. He fell to his knees, groping blindly ahead. His arms wrapped around a pair of legs, clung there grimly. Something lashed out at his chest, spilling him over on his back.

"Alan, where are you?" Eugene Talbrick said. "What's the matter?" Then Eugene Talbrick screamed once and was still. A weight fell across Alan, pinning him to the floor. Half-conscious, he rolled the heavy thing off him and scrambled unsteadily to his hands and knees. The door opened and closed swiftly, light from the corridor streaming in, then fading. Alan staggered to the door, opened it.

Outside in the corridor, there was no one.

Inside, the slender form of Eugene Talbrick was stretched out on its back. A red pool of blood was spreading on the carpet under him. Alan knew he was dead without feeling for the pulse.

A knife had been plunged into Eugene Talbrick's side, immediately below the heart.

CHAPTER THREE

"NOW, just a minute, Alan," Bennett Keifer said later. "Before you go off half-cocked like that—"

"Eugene made some accusations, then died," Alan insisted, "before he could show me the proof."

"We're all grownups here, Alan," Keifer said easily. There was no mistaking his tone. He would assume Alan was a grownup. "You're twenty-five," he went on. "One day soon you'll take over the Federation movement, so you can't afford to be impetuous. You tried to find that letter, didn't you?"

"Yes," Alan admitted. "It wasn't there."

"Of course it wasn't. It never existed. Alan, listen to me. Talbrick was an old man. Our viewpoints differed diametrically. He couldn't reconcile himself with the fact that your father agreed with me."

"But—"

"But that isn't important. This is. Someone, some unknown person, killed your father. Someone killed Talbrick. Richard Tremaine, then Talbrick. I'm next in line, Alan. Or maybe you are. Someone is out to wreck the Federation from the inside, by killing off its leaders."

"If what you say is true, why didn't they finish the job in Talbrick's apartment? They could have killed me, too."

"You frightened them off."

"I'll be frank," Alan said coolly. "Let's assume you were responsible. You couldn't afford to kill me. You need me for a figurehead."

Keifer smiled. "I should be angry. I'm not." He flipped the intercom toggle on his desk and said, "Haddix, come in here, please."

The door opened. A tall, gangling man in the uniform of a Federation captain entered the room. He moved with easy, feline grace. When he spoke, he purred like a great cat. "Yes, sir?" he said saluting Keifer. "You sent for me?"

"Alan, this is Captain Haddix, the Internal Security Officer here at Red Sands. Captain, will you tell Mr. Tremaine where I was for the past three hours?"

"Right here, sir. You had a brief interview with this man, then remained here with me, discussing the water ultimatum."

"You see?" Keifer said. "Right here."

Perhaps he had jumped to an unwarranted conclusion, Alan thought. He said, "What is this water ultimatum?"

Keifer dismissed the Internal Security Officer, then explained, "We're in trouble, Alan. An hour ago, the Earth colonial office contacted us with an ultimatum. Either we lay down our arms and tell the provisional governments on the other Outworlds to surrender their authority, or Mars' water supply is cut off. We were given one hour."

"But Earth's own military forces here on Mars would die of thirst."

Keifer shrugged. "Apparently they're expendable. Of course, I rejected the ultimatum."

"What can you do?"

"I don't know," Keifer said. "They can do what they say, unfortunately."

It would be simple, Alan knew. Arid Mars had depended for water, which flowed in an adequate trickle from the polar caps, until the coming of the Earth colony. For the past twenty years, though, water-surplus Venus supplied Mars with its water. A warp had been opened in space from the Venusian orbit to the Martian, with life-giving water flowing through from the second planet to the fourth at the rate of fifty thousand gallons per second. It had been a stupendous sub-space engineering feat, for the warp varied in length from sixty to two-hundred million miles, depending upon the orbital positions of the two planets. Earth could shut the warp at any point along its vast length. Parched, arid Mars would be forced to lay down its arms in a matter of days.

"Captain Haddix is taking a ship along the warp-route," Keifer said, "assuming the ultimatum is in earnest. He might be able to find the break, but I doubt if he could repair it. Would you care to go along?"

"Yes," Alan said. He still didn't believe Earth would subject millions of people, its own military garrison included, to a killing thirst.

"Very well. I—"

At that moment a buzzer sounded on Keifer's desk. "Yes, what is it?"

The voice was frantic. "This is the reservoir, sir. The water's stopped flowing. The warp is closed!"

"We'll ration what we have left," Keifer said grimly. "Two quarts per person, effective immediately." Then, to Alan: "I'll make arrangements for you with Captain Haddix. They weren't fooling, Alan. They gave us exactly one hour."

Alan met Captain Haddix outside, where plans were made for their flight to the space warp route. If Earth did this, Alan thought bleakly, then maybe Keifer was right. For Earth would thereby condemn itself in the eyes of the Outworlds with such blatant disregard for human life.

"THEY haven't touched us so far, Dad," Laura Olmstead told her father. "Alan won't let them."

"We're prisoners in this room. But I think Alan's a prisoner, too. Up here." General Olmstead tapped his head.

"They've got the boy fooled, Laura, if what you told me is the truth."

"I'm sure it is. I'm sure Alan wouldn't have betrayed his own father like that. You've got to trust him, Dad."

General Olmstead grunted. "We don't have any choice, do we?"

Laura was thinking: *Please, Alan. Please. They've got you confused. You didn't do this intentionally. Please.*

The door to their prison chamber suddenly slid, with much grating and creaking, into the wall. A tall, distinguished-looking man in the uniform of a Federation colonel came into the room. "I am Colonel Bennett Keifer," he introduced himself, "second in command to Alan Tremaine here at Red Sands. How do you do, Mr. Olmstead?"

"*General* Olmstead," Laura's father said coldly.

"We recognize no Earth titles here in Red Sands, Mr. Olmstead. We recognize your importance, though."

"Exactly what does that mean?"

"There are certain things Alan Tremaine would like to find out. The strength of the Earth garrison at Syrtis Major, the number of jet-copters at your disposal, your plans for putting down the insurrections at the smaller Martian settlements."

"You'll get nothing from me," General Olmstead promised.

"Perhaps. Your daughter is a lovely woman, Mr. Olmstead. Quite lovely."

"If you as much as touch her, I'll kill you with my own hands…"

"Theatrics, Mr. Olmstead. You are in no position to do anything of the sort. You can save us both a lot of trouble if you answer my questions."

"Get out of here," General Olmstead said.

Shrugging, Keifer called over his shoulder: "Guard!"

Two strapping figures entered the chamber and waited for orders.

"Take Mr. Olmstead to another room, please. I wish you were more reasonable, Mr. Olmstead. We need that information badly."

STRUGGLING and cursing, General Olmstead was borne from the room. "Don't worry about me," Laura called after him. "We both have a duty to Earth."

"This is ironic," Keifer said after the door had closed. "I had planned it thoroughly. We have men here who are experts in an art that was old when civilization was young."

"Torture?" Laura said. "My father won't—"

"I said it's ironic. I never expected you, Laura. The General has a daughter, a common, ordinary girl. He loves her. He sees things in her no one else does. But you—you are beautiful. Listen to me, Laura. Your father is an experienced professional soldier. We can use him here in Red Sands. If we make an alliance, the Federation could hold all of Mars in a week."

"What kind of alliance?"

"There are few women in Red Sands," said Keifer. "None of them as pretty as you. I'm restless, Laura. That kind of alliance." Quite objectively, he let his eyes study her slowly, starting at the top of her head and working down without passion, without hurry. When he finished, she was blushing. "Exactly that kind of an alliance," he said.

"You're crazy if you think I—"

"Your father expects the worst. He thinks we're going to hurt you. We're not. We're going to hurt him.

"Plans can change. Your father will be tortured, while you are sitting here with me. We can break a man, Laura, physically and mentally. We can make him talk. Or—you can save us the trouble."

"How?"

"By telling your father you believe this is the winning side. By telling him you're going to live with me."

"To—what?"

"To live with me."

"I wouldn't marry you if—"

"My dear young lady. I never said anything about marriage. Perhaps later, I don't know. I'm a cautious man. You're still an unknown quantity, you see."

"You can just get out of here."

"As you wish. But let me tell you something...here in Red Sands we're subtle when we have to be, crude when we must. Now, take your father. There are ways of hurting a man, of pulling out his fingernails slowly, of applying pressure to certain nerves at the base of the skull, of a slow, steady pounding of the soles of the feet, of breaking bones, starting with the toes and—"

"That's enough!" Laura cried. "Don't say any more."

Keifer shrugged. "Also as you wish. Your father will not be harmed. I promise you. Tonight, you may come to my quarters if you wish. If you don't my promise will no longer be valid. In a day or two, perhaps we can tell your father of our alliance. Will I see you tonight?"

"Yes," Laura said. "Just get out of here now."

"Tonight," Keifer told her, and left the room.

CHAPTER FOUR

"THIS is Colonel Keifer calling warp-ship seven. Come in please."

"Warp seven, sir."

"Captain Haddix?"

"Just a moment, sir."

Keifer waited impatiently, then saw Haddix's gaunt face on the viewscreen. "Where are you now, Haddix?"

"Starting out along the warp-route, sir. Has there been a change in plans?"

"Yes. I want you to return tonight, Captain Haddix. Without Alan Tremaine."

"But I thought—"

"Don't. We still need Tremaine's name, but the boy is suspicious. No one has to know he has been killed. This is one case where we want the name but not the game. You understand?"

"Yes, sir."

"One more thing, Captain. How would you like to attain your majority?"

"Yes, *sir...*" Haddix beamed.

"Good. Return tonight without Tremaine and you'll be promoted. Good luck, Captain."

*   *   *

Alan felt awkward in the cumbersome spacesuit, clamping along the hull of warp ship seven with Captain Haddix. Ahead of him, Haddix looked like some grotesque monster in the shapeless, inflated suit. But Haddix had learned to slide his feet along in their magnet-shod boots and could move with comparative ease.

"There's the warp station," Haddix called over the suit intercom, pointing with one gauntleted hand toward a black globe that obscured the starlight overhead. From the globe, an incredibly straight black line darted out across the gulf of space like a bridge to infinity. From here it seemed only inches thick, but Alan knew it was actually fifty feet across.

"That's the warp," Haddix said. "It bends space as if space were a sheet of paper with Venus at one corner and Mars at another. You fold the sheet of paper across to place Venus and Mars in juxtaposition. In the same way, this warp folds space, aligning Venus and Mars in sub-space."

"Why can't men travel the same way?" Alan asked. "It's almost instantaneous, isn't it? It takes almost a month by spaceship from Mars to Venus."

Haddix's laughter purred over the intercom. "Uh-uh," he said. "The stresses in a space-warp are tremendous. Water has no shape to lose, so it doesn't matter. A man would be mangled. Well, are you ready, Mr. Tremaine?"

"I guess so."

"Fine. Just point yourself in the direction of the warp station, unmagnetize your boots and switch on your shoulder jets. Once you get the hang of it, it's a cinch. Here we go."

Ahead of him, Alan saw Haddix's form suddenly lift from the hull of the spaceship and rocket up toward the warp station. Alan followed him, feeling utterly no sensation of movement after the initial acceleration.

A FEATURELESS black globe several hundred yards in diameter, the warp station floated toward them. Following Haddix's lead, Alan alighted on his hands, cutting his shoulder jets and cartwheeling into an upright position. The warp-station, he knew, was merely a terminal point for the space-warp itself. Untended, it housed the tremendous atomic power plant that unfolded the water on the Martian end of the warp from sub-space to normal space.

"As you can see," Haddix said, "the station is working. But there's no water."

Alan could feel the pulsing of great machinery underfoot. But the black tube of sub-space, yawning awesomely half a hundred feet to his left, was empty.

"Want to take a look?" Haddix asked.

Alan nodded through the glassite helmet of his space suit, then fell into dragging, magnetized step beside Haddix. Soon they approached the lip of the sub-space tube, where sub-space intersected normal space in a fifty-foot wide channel.

"It doesn't look dangerous," Alan said.

"For water, it's not. The pressure would crush a man to jelly."

Alan peered over the edge. Below him perhaps a dozen feet, a white line had been painted. Over it in stark white letters was the word CAUTION. Beyond that point, apparently, the actual space warp began.

"Look out!" Alan shouted. "What are you trying to do?"

Haddix was leaning against him, their two bulky suits in sudden, dangerous contact. Alan could feel himself slipping over the edge. Yelling now, his own voice deafening him inside the glassite helmet, Alan groped with clumsy, gauntleted hands for Haddix. He clutched the shoulder of the man's space suit, then felt himself tumbling over the edge into the tube.

There was a jolting sensation above him. He was sliding down the inflated body of Haddix's spacesuit, sliding, sliding. He wrapped his arms about the legs of the suit and clung there. Below his dangling feet was the white line and the word CAUTION painted there, immediately below that, the space-warp itself.

"Let go of me! Haddix screamed. "You'll kill us both."

Alan looked up. Haddix was clinging to the lip of the tube with both hands. Suddenly, Haddix began rocking back and forth in an attempt to dislodge Alan.

"Don't try it," Alan said. "All I've got to do is yank at your legs a little harder and we'll both fall down there."

"I can't climb up with you hanging on like that. I—I can't hold on much longer. This warp-station's at Earth normal gravity, Tremaine. My hands are slipping!"

"Listen to me," Alan said. "We can still get out of this. I can climb up your back, then pull you up after me."

"How do I know you will?"

"You don't. If we just hang here, we're as good as dead." Alan could feel the strain in his arms as he clung to Haddix's suit. For Haddix, the strain was double. Haddix could not be expected to hang there more than a few moments.

"I'm coming up," Alan said. "Don't try anything foolish."

HANGING by one arm, Alan reached up with his other hand and grasped the belt of Haddix's suit. Suspended there by both arms now, he reached up again for the flange of metal at the neck of Haddix's suit, where the glassite helmet fit. He got the gauntleted fingers of one hand around it, then almost lost his precarious grip. He swung sickeningly over the abyss for one harrowing moment, then held the flange with both hands. Taking a deep breath, he reached for the lip of the tube itself and soon clambered up and over. He lay there briefly, panting. He had never been nearer death in his life.

"Help!" Haddix gasped. "I can't hold on much longer."

Alan crouched there, looked over the edge. Haddix still clung with both hands.

"Why did you try to kill me?" Alan demanded. "Did you kill my father and Eugene Talbrick too?"

"It was Keifer!" Haddix cried. "Keifer thought you were suspicious. He was going to get you out of the way and keep using your name."

"Did he kill my father?"

"I don't know. Honest."

"And Talbrick?"

"One of my men did it. At Keifer's orders. Get me out of here. I'm begging you."

"Okay," Alan said. He braced himself and hauled Haddix up out of the tube, then turned and jetted back toward the waiting warp-ship. They entered the airlock together, waited for the green safety light that announced the return of normal pressure and air, then stripped off their deflated spacesuits and glassite helmets.

Cat-quick, Haddix yanked an atomic pistol from his belt.

Instinctively, matching reflex for reflex, Alan slapped it from his hand. The weapon roared, blasting the air over Alan's head as he dove for Haddix. They went down together, rolling across the floor. Alan was aware of Haddix shouting for help, of the Captain's long fingers closing on his throat, of a knee driven painfully into his groin.

The inner lock door swung open. The warp-ship's pilot crashed through and scrambled on the floor after the atomic pistol. "Get out of the way, Captain," he said. "I've got him covered."

But Haddix was a growling, choking, feline animal now, trying to squeeze the life from Alan's throat. Desperately, Alan groped blindly with his fingers. His thumbs found Haddix's eyes, gouging. Haddix screamed and tumbled clear, clawing at his face.

Alan sucked air into his lungs and sprang to his feet as the atomic pistol was discharged. He felt a sudden, burning numbness in his left arm, then was grappling with the pilot chest to chest, the atomic pistol between them. When the weapon went off, Alan was flung across the airlock, slamming against the wall. The pilot went down to his knees slowly, disbelief on his face as he died trying to stuff entrails back into his belly.

Haddix and Alan went for the atomic pistol at the same time. The Security Officer got his fingers around it and turned, snarling, toward Alan.

"All right, you no good son—" he began.

Alan stepped on his wrist, pinning it on the floor with the weapon. He kicked Haddix in the face with his other foot and retrieved the atomic pistol as Haddix slumped forward.

"Now listen," Alan said breathing in great sobs, "we're going forward. You'll call Keifer and tell him I'm dead. Try anything else and I'll kill you. Understand?"

Haddix understood.

Alan followed him, stuffing his numb left hand into a pocket of his blouse as a temporary sling. By the time they reached the control cabin, the left side of his blouse was soaked with blood.

"GOOD dinner, wasn't it?" Bennett Keifer asked Laura.

"Yes," she said.

"Did you like the wine?"

"Yes."

"I'm glad you decided to accept my invitation. Are you?"

"Yes."

"Is that all you have to say 'yes'?"

"What do you want me to say?"

"Come here. Laura."

Dad, she thought. *It's for you. Alan, Alan, where are you?* She walked to where Keifer was sitting.

"Sit down, Laura."

She sat.

"You still don't like me," he said, as if it were both regretted and unexpected. "But you're all alone now. I've given you the opportunity to start a new life here with me. Your father can't help you. And Alan Tremaine—"

"What about Alan?" Laura asked eagerly.

"I want ours to be a frank relationship. No lies. No deceits. Alan Tremaine is dead."

"What—what did you say?" Laura cried.

"Tremaine is dead. I got word this afternoon. An accident at the warp-station."

"It isn't true," Laura whispered. "It can't he true. Please. Please…"

"Listen to me, Laura. I'm going to win. I can't be stopped now. I'm offering you half, a woman's share of empire. Not just the Outworlds. I believe I can force Earth itself to its knees."

Alan, Alan, forgive me. I said I hated you…

"It isn't madness, Laura. With Tremaine's name and my plans, the Outworlds will rally behind me. And after they hear how Earth has sundered the space-warp from Venus—"

"Earth wouldn't," Laura said mechanically.

"It's on every Martian's lips," Keifer said.

"Then you did it yourself."

"Laura, Laura. I said a woman's share of empire. Don't worry yourself over the details. Wealth and jewels and importance, that's a woman's share. It's yours if you want it."

"My father—"

"Is a prisoner. Will you come here now?"

Laura looked at him, at this man who would carve a solar empire for himself by twisting the legitimate motives of the Outworld people. *It's for Dad,* she thought. She tried to fill her mind with that and nothing else. For her father.

Otherwise, he would be tortured. For her father. For her father...

But when Keifer smiled down on her, calmly sure of himself, she thought of other things, of Earth, which did not yet understand the full extent of Keifer's madness, and of Alan, who had been slain treacherously...

"That's for my father!" she cried, and slapped Keifer's face.

He caught her hands, pinning them at her side. "You little vixen," he said. The imprints of her fingers were on his cheek. There was quick hatred in his eyes, but lust as well. "Why don't you cry for help?" he taunted her. "My guards will hear you."

Laura freed one of her hands and slapped him again, then watched as rage swept the lust from his eyes. "I'll break you," he promised, biting off the words one at a time. "You'll come crawling." He forced her down slowly on the couch.

They both looked up as the door to the room slid noisily into the wall.

Alan stood there.

CHAPTER FIVE

"GET up," Alan said, jerking the atomic pistol from his belt.

"But Haddix said—"

"Your guards welcomed me, Keifer. You couldn't afford to tell anyone else I was dead. Laura, are you all right?"

"Yes, Alan. I thought you...he said..."

"We're getting out of here. Keifer, call your guards. Tell them to bring General Olmstead here. If you try any tricks, I'll kill you." Alan's head was whirling. He'd lost too much blood, he thought vaguely. There were two Laura's, and two Keifer's swimming before his eyes.

"You can't desert your own people," Keifer told him. You don't like my policies, but—"

"Shut up. You told Haddix to kill me. One of Haddix's men killed Eugene Talbrick, at your orders."

"I—"

Alan jammed the atomic pistol against Keifer's chest. "One question," he said. "I want the truth. Who cut off the space-warp?"

"Earth—"

"I'm going to Earth to find out. I just want to know where I stand that's all."

Keifer shrugged. "We did it, Alan. The Federation."

"You mean *you* did it. But why?"

Keifer remained stonily silent.

Abruptly, Alan found himself down on one knee. It took an incredible effort of will to stand up again. He needed a blood transfusion and could sleep around the clock and still wake up exhausted. Laura ran to him and said, "You're badly hurt, Alan. You ought to have that treated."

He smiled bleakly. "Tell me how?" he said, and handed her the pistol. "If Keifer does anything except send for your father use this."

He staggered to the couch and sat there, letting his head slump forward and down almost to his knees to renew the flow of blood to his brain. Dimly, he was aware of Keifer crossing the room to a video screen and asking someone at the other end to bring General Olmstead—Keifer said *Mr.* Olmstead—to his quarters.

Then there was a roaring in Alan's ears, the distant, far off pounding of surf on a water world like Venus, not arid Mars. It came closer; it swept down upon Alan in a surging, foaming tide and engulfed him.

"ALAN! Alan! Dad is here."

"Laura..." He blinked his eyes. Groggy, he stood up. Laura was on one side of him, General Olmstead on the other pointing the atomic pistol squarely at Bennett Keifer.

"Just how do you expect to get out of here?" Keifer demanded.

"That's easy," Alan said. "You are coming with us."

"To Earth? You'll never make me."

"Get this straight," Alan said. "I could walk clear across Red Sands without anyone trying to stop me. I'm Alan Tremaine, remember? But we're going to do it the hard way because I want to turn you over to the authorities on Earth. Let's go."

Outside in the corridor, a few guards were loitering. They came to attention and saluted smartly as Keifer and Alan Tremaine came into view with General Olmstead and his daughter. They never suspected that General Olmstead held a pistol, hidden by the folds of his tunic, at Keifer's back.

General Olmstead told Alan as they followed the narrow corridor to a larger one. "My place is with the defenders of Red Sands. I wouldn't feel right going to Earth with you."

"We're taking the warp-ship," Alan said. "It's not really built for interplanetary travel, but it will have to do. We could drop you at Syrtis. But sir, I'd rather take Laura with me. Let's get her safely out of this war."

"Wait a minute!" Laura cried. "If you think—"

"I do," her father said, "and so does Alan. You'll go to Earth with him. He needs someone along to help watch Keifer, anyhow."

"But Dad—"

"But nothing."

"Alan, I want to go with you, but—"

"You heard your father. But nothing."

Fifteen minutes later, they were putting on insulined surface garments at the quartermaster supply depot near the great stone portal that separated Red Sands from the Martian desert.

The clerk said, "Going up to the warp-station?"

"No," Bennett Keifer told him.

"Yes," Alan said.

The clerk scratched his head, but saluted as they marched toward the stone portal. "Open it," Alan told him.

The portal slid away. The fierce Martian wind blasted them with swirling, choking sand. The intense cold cleared Alan's head. Five hundred yards across the ochre sand, they could see the black bulk of the warp ship. The portal groaned and scraped shut behind them. You could see nothing but a bare escarpment of Martian granite.

"Haddix is tied up in the ship," Alan shouted over the shrieking wind. "We'll put him outside, then blast off."

Now the warp ship loomed over them, balanced black and ugly on its tail. Alan worked the airlock mechanism with numb fingers. The lock swung in.

Haddix was there, all right. Haddix stood in the airlock with another uniformed figure on either side of him.

Haddix was pointing an atomic pistol out at them.

"HE left me here," Haddix told Keifer. "I got loose and called for help. I figured he was planning to use the ship again or he would have taken me out with him. So we waited right here. Smart, huh?"

"That was ingenious, *Major* Haddix," Keifer agreed.

Haddix climbed out of the airlock and stood with them on the ochre sand. His two men emerged behind him with coils of rope. "Sit down." Haddix said, "A trick I learned on Venus. We'll tie them back to back."

Nodding, Keifer asked General Olmstead for his weapon.

Alan crouched, facing Haddix. Once they were tied, they were as good as dead. Rallying the Outworld people behind Alan's name, Keifer would certainly dominate the Federation planets and might even go further. Haddix stood there warily, feet planted wide apart, ready for anything. It hardly seemed a calculated risk Alan thought. It seemed like suicide.

But there was nothing else he could do.

He scooped up a handful of sand and flung it in Haddix's face, leaping for the Security Officer with the same motion. Then several things happened at once. Laura screamed. Keifer was grappling with General Olmstead, fighting a grim tug of war with him for the pistol. Haddix's weapon blasted air just above Alan's face, the searing flash of energy momentarily blinding him. Alan hit Haddix low with his shoulder, striking the man's knees, he thought. Haddix tumbled over on top of him, flattening Alan against the sand.

Alan got two handfuls of sand, then drove his fists at Haddix's face and opened them, rubbing the sand into his eyes. Haddix screamed like an animal in sudden, unexpected pain. There was a sudden wet warmth on Alan's left arm as the wound opened and began bleeding again, but Haddix had fallen away from him and Alan's energy-blinded eyes were beginning to make out shapes again.

He found Haddix's weapon in his hand as the two soldiers charged down upon him. He fired once and blasted a hole in the first one's chest. Haddix was scrambling over the sand toward him, groping blindly, cursing. The second soldier swung his coil of rope like a flail, whipping it down across Alan's face. He felt blood flowing in a quick torrent from his nose. He held the atomic pistol in both hands as the soldier lifted the rope overhead again. The second blast of energy from Alan's weapon decapitated the soldier. The head tumbled away. The body took two steps toward Alan as if it could not believe this had happened, then pitched forward on the sand, staining the ochre with a deeper red.

Alan gagged but did not have time to be sick. He stood up and saw Haddix fleeing toward the escarpment that hid Red Sands. He fired once, but the range was too great, the wind too strong. Keifer and Laura were fighting for the second atomic pistol, Laura kicking him, raking his face with her fingernails and keeping him away from General Olmstead, who lay motionless on the sand. Keifer struck her brutally across the jaw with his fist, then turned, fired once in Alan's direction without aiming, and sprinted toward the escarpment.

Laura was unconscious. General Olmstead was unconscious or dead. Alan's limbs were like water. He knew Keifer would bring help. He had perhaps three minutes.

Somehow, he managed to drag Laura and her father inside the warp ship. He slammed the outer airlock door, closed the inner door, staggered to the controls. Figures, tiny black dots against the barren ochre wilderness, were running toward the ship when Alan took it up into space under five G's acceleration.

Everything was going to be all right, he thought, and fainted.

SOMETHING cool was stroking his forehead, bathing the caked blood from his face. He was aware that his tunic and blouse had been removed, aware of a clean white bandage on his arm. Laura's face swam in and out of focus before him.

"Where are we?" he asked.

Laura did not answer.

He looked at the controls. Seventy five thousand miles out from Mars, heading toward Earth. Present speed, thirty eight miles per second, still increasing. He could feel the gentle acceleration pressure, probably one-and-a-half G's, tugging at him.

"Are we being followed?" he asked Laura.

"No. I don't know. Please. Please!"

"What's the matter?"

"Dad. He's—dead, Alan. Keifer killed him." Laura was crying silently, her shoulder shaking with sobs, her eyelids closed tightly, the tears streaming from them down her cheeks. "He's—dead..."

Alan stood up and walked to where he had dragged General Olmstead's inert form. A hole in the General's tunic revealed the wound. There was no pulse beat in his wrist.

First my father, Alan thought. First Richard Tremaine. Now General Olmstead. They were on opposite sides, the one championing freedom for the Outworlds, the other opposing it. But there had been nothing violent about their disagreement. It had been a political battle, waged in the arena of politics. And when Richard Tremaine had been granted Equal Union for his people, General Olmstead had bowed graciously to Earth's decision. Under other circumstances, they could have been friends, Alan's dead father and Laura's.

Now they were dead.

Both struck down by Bennett Keifer.

Alan wondered if it was always that way. The bad people rising to the top, like scum on water, employing treachery and violence to achieve their ends.

"It will be more than a vendetta," he said out loud.

"What did you say?"

"I'm going to get Keifer. My whole life will stand still until I can get him. Not because he killed them, not entirely for that. Because of who he is and what he stands for and how he'll use treachery and violence like this for his own ends. Because Equal Union and parliamentary routine never satisfied a man like him and never will. Because he can stop the flow of water to Mars and watch his own people crying for water if it serves his purposes to incite them against Earth. I'll get him, Laura. I promise you that."

He wrapped General Olmstead's body in an old Federation flag, which he found in a rear cabin of the warp-ship. "It isn't the globe and stars of Earth," he said softly, "but it's the Federation my father stood for, the real Federation."

Laura nodded. "Dad would have wanted it that way."

Alan carried his flag-draped burden to the airlock, placed it in the chamber, then stepped back and bolted the inner door. Laura stood silently for a moment with her head bowed while Alan recited what he could remember of the 23rd Psalm. Somehow, it cleaned some of the hatred from his system and left cold clear purpose in its place. The prayer was for his father too and all the free people who had ever died and would ever die fighting tyranny.

"Though I walk through the valley of the shadow of death I shall fear no evil, for Thou art with me. Thy rod and Thy staff, they comfort me…

Alan pulled the lever that controlled the outer door of the airlock. General Olmstead found his final resting-place in the deep void of space where he had spent most of his life in the service of his fellow men.

CHAPTER SIX

"FIVE hundred thousand miles out from Earth," Laura said, two weeks later.

"I still don't get it," Alan admitted. "They didn't even try to follow us. It's as if Keifer suddenly didn't care whether we escaped to Earth or not."

"Maybe he believes we're going to have our hands full trying to get Earth to repair the space-warp. Maybe he knows we won't be able to bother him or interfere with his plans."

But Alan shook his head, his brow creasing into a frown. "No that's not it. I just can't figure it." He walked to the fore viewport and gazed at the legions of stars against the black velvet immensity of space. In the upper right hand corner of the viewport he could see the Earth-moon system, the larger sphere pale green, mottled with white and brown, the smaller a dazzling white. He realized all at once that he had two homes. The Mars of his boyhood, the Earth and New Washington University, where he had spent his young manhood. He could never forsake one for the other. He was as much of Earth as he was of Mars, the verdant green richness of the one tugging at him with no less force than the arid, wild frontier of the other.

"See if you can get anything on the radio," he told Laura. The warp ship's receiver was a small one not meant for interplanetary distances, but Alan guessed it could pick up the more powerful Earth stations beamed to space through the Heavyside Layer.

The radio squawked and whistled, and then they heard an announcer's voice faintly. "...of Alan Tremaine's Federation forces. All Earth is still shocked over Tremaine's ultimatum. The International Security Council has been meeting in closed session for two days now, with no announced decisions.

"Authoritative sources close to the Council say that President Holland has admitted the Earth is helpless. It has been known for more than a century that man's science was capable of building a cobalt bomb that, with a weight of perhaps four hundred tons, could poison all life on Earth with radioactivity.

"As we all have known since last Wednesday, this is precisely what Tremaine has in mind. The cobalt bomb is actually a hydrogen bomb with a layer of cobalt isotope surrounding it. While radioactive cobalt tritium from the H-bomb trigger is quickly dispersed and rendered harmless because the half-life of tritium is so short, radioactive cobalt can spread through the Earth's upper atmosphere on the jet stream, raining lethal gamma rays from pole to pole.

"It is this terrible force that Alan Tremaine has threatened to unleash on the Earth."

"That's a lie!" Laura cried. "You are not even there. It's Keifer, using your name."

Alan nodded grimly. "He couldn't give such an ultimatum himself. The Outworld people wouldn't listen. But if they believe it's my decision…"

The commentator was saying: "…brief review of the points of Tremaine's ultimatum. One, unconditional surrender of all remaining Earth forces on the Outworlds. Two, repair of the space warp bringing water from Venus to Mars. Tremaine claims Earth broke the warp, but the government has denied this right along. It is believed Tremaine is instilling hatred for Earth in the Federation peoples with this diabolical lie. Three, total independence for Outworlds. Four, Tremaine threatens that if the first three conditions are not complied with by tomorrow night, twenty-three hundred hours Greenwich Time, he will unleash the cobalt bomb.

"Since Tremaine's Federation has sundered the space-warp itself, Earth is unable to comply with the second of Tremaine's points. While radar defenses are being alerted on a planet-wide basis, an unmanned rocket with a cobalt-bomb warhead, approaching the Earth at interplanetary speeds, could not be stopped. The Earth government has continued its hourly appeal to Tremaine not to destroy the civilization that has carried mankind out to the planets. So far, Tremaine has not responded."

"He—he wouldn't dare," Laura said as Alan shut the radio. But her voice lacked conviction.

"He might, Laura. He just might do anything. The radioactivity wouldn't last forever. Keifer might be planning to wait until it's dispersed, then return to Earth and extend his plans for empire there. All life would die, but he could replant crops, bring his hand-picked leaders to settle with him, and govern the solar system as a small totalitarian state."

"But I thought he wanted to take over Earth and all its people."

"He might figure they won't listen to him. If they do, he takes over. If they don't, he goes through with his ultimatum. Either way, he has Earth."

"But Alan. Five billion people…"

"I'm going down there," Alan said. "I've got to find out all the details."

"Alan, they'll kill you! They think it's your ultimatum, your cobalt bomb."

"If anyone can stop Keifer, I can. The Federation is loyal to me."

"They won't listen to you. They won't let you talk. They'll kill you."

"My father died for what he believed," Alan said. "So did your father. As long as there's a chance, I've got to go down there. Keifer's ultimatum is set for tomorrow night."

IMPULSIVELY, Laura took his hands and squeezed them. "I won't let you throw your life away. I can't lose you now, Alan. I can't. I..."

Alan tilted her chin with his hand and looked into her eyes. Her lips were trembling. She was going to cry, he thought. "Darling," he said, "you've got to listen. I love you. I...I think I was falling in love with you on the Mars liner, before all this started to happen. I never had a chance to tell you. I'm telling you now."

"Then you can't..."

Their lips came together, gently at first, then fiercely, as if this were their first kiss of love and perhaps their last. "Oh, Alan. Yes, Alan. I love you. So you can't..."

"No," Alan told her quietly. "I've got to. Once a great poet of Earth put it so clearly, so much better than I could ever say it. "How did it go? Something about 'I could not love thee, dear, so much, lov'd I not honor more.' Do you think for a minute we could live with ourselves or ever look each other in the eye again if we let this happen without trying to stop it?"

"I'm begging you, Alan. They will kill you as soon as you set foot on Earth."

"I said I'm going down there. I am going. But not before I convince you." He spoke long and persuasively. He told her about other lovers, everywhere, about the men and women of Earth, the five billion helpless people who had a right to live their own lives too and fall in love and marry, about the hundreds of millions of Outworlders whose minds and hearts would be fettered by Bennett Keifer if he had his way, about how a man had this double allegiance all his life, to the people he loved and to freedom and democracy and the ideas in which he believed. How the one allegiance might make a man think of an island somewhere or a small asteroid where the rest of the world wouldn't matter but how the other allegiance always brought him back to the crowded places, the dangerous places.

Laura kissed him again, sobbing, clinging to him. When finally he let her go, she whispered so low he hardly could hear the words: "You are right, Alan. It's your duty to go."

"Whatever happens, Laura, I love you."

"Keep telling me that all the time, Alan. I don't want to hear anything else. I'm going with you."

He smiled, then shook his head. "You're going to Earth all right. But you're going where you'll be safe."

Then Alan took the ship down, watching the great green globe of Earth swelling up toward them and then the wondrous sight of the continents swimming into view and the vast blue-green seas and the white cottony puffs of cloud formations and wondering if he soon would be saying goodbye to Laura for the last time.

IT was night In New Washington. Outside, you could hear the familiar street sounds, the jet-cars rushing by, the muted talk of people after the theater down the street closed for the night, the gentle sighing of wind in the trees which spanned the avenue.

Inside the fraternity lodge, everything was quiet. New Washington students were studying in their small rooms; some of them had already retired. Bill Graham, who had been Alan's roommate in the good days, said: "You know I want to believe you, Alan. We've been friends ever since we started through college together."

"All I want you to do is watch Laura. Don't let her out of your sight."

"But everyone says you gave Earth the ultimatum."

"Would I be here now if I did? I'm trying to prevent it, Bill. You've got to believe me."

"All I have to do is watch her?"

"Yes. I'm going straight to the President if I can. Something's been bothering me about this ultimatum of Keifer's all along. Now I think I know what it is. I think we have a chance to stop him, Bill. Just a chance, but we can try."

"What about your ship? How did you get through the radar net?"

Alan smiled grimly. "I remembered your registration number, Bill. I had to give it to them. They'll think it was your ship."

"Holy Mac!" Bill Graham cried. "Then they'll think I—"

"If Keifer wins, we'll all be dead tomorrow night anyway. It was the only thing I could do Bill. I had to get through."

Bill Graham chuckled softly, as if it all were very funny. But he reached out and shook Alan's hand. "I'll watch her, Alan."

Alan nodded, turned to Laura and kissed her quickly without saying goodbye. That way, he thought, he had to see her again...

Everything was so normal on the streets of New Washington, it almost made Alan think that the Federation uprising, the death of his father and Laura's father, and Keifer's ultimatum to Earth, were all part of some wild, impossible dream. The boys and girls were walking hand in hand. The old men were walking their dogs or taking their evening constitutionals or stopping on street corners to talk with their friends. The theater marquees were gay and well lighted. It was only when you studied the faces and saw the lines of worry, the furrowed brows, the thoughtful, furtive looks, only when you listened to the conversations and heard

"Tremaine's ultimatum"…"nothing at all we can do"…"he wouldn't dare"…"helpless"…"I'm going to pretend nothing's wrong and just go right on living till tomorrow night"…"what else can you do?"…"dear God, what else?"…it was only then that you knew.

Alan took a bus to the center or the city and fell in with a group of reporters converging on the White House. One of them was saying, "About time they let us in on this. That International Security Council hasn't uttered a peep since the ultimatum, but they've been meeting continuously."

"Ought to make a few banner headlines," another man said.

"So what? After tomorrow night, there won't be any more headlines—or anything. If I could just get that Tremaine here, how I'd love to choke the life out of him with these two hands.'"

"You and about five billion other people."

THEY entered the White House grounds. Ahead of them, the stately white building was ablaze with light. Guards were stationed at all the entrances.

The reporters began to queue up in single file as two uniformed men examined their credentials. His heart pounding, Alan let the line carry him forward. All the doors were guarded. If he could not get in this way, he could not get in at all.

Finally, he was saying: "Adams, New York Times."

"Your press card, Mr. Adams?"

"I left it at the hotel."

The guard shook his head. "Sorry. You'll have to get it."

"I don't want to miss the press conference."

The guard looked up and shouted, "Anyone else from the New York Times here?"

A man behind Alan nodded.

"You know this fellow?"

The man studied Alan, then shrugged. "Don't think so. I never forget a face."

"He says he's from the Times."

"The devil he is."

"Who are you?" the guard asked Alan.

For answer, Alan shoved him out of the way and plunged inside the building. His feet pounded a loud tattoo on the polished marble floor as he sprinted down the corridor. There were shouts and the pounding of more feet behind him. He followed an arrow that pointed straight ahead above the words PRESS ROOM. He climbed a broad marble staircase. The voices were louder behind him, the click-clacking feet closer.

Breathing harshly, he charged through the doorway to the press gallery. He stopped in his tracks.

The International Security Council was assembled in special session, ready to meet the reporters and their questions. Alan recognized the faces, the gaunt, weary but somehow intensely warm features of President Holland, the other races, all grave and tired, about the horseshoe-shaped table.

The guards sprinted up behind Alan, pinning his arms to his sides.

The Secretary General of the International Security Council, seated at President Holland's right, looked up and said, "What is the trouble here?"

"Begging your pardon, sir," the first guard explained, "this man has no proper identification."

President Holland glanced up at Alan, the deep-set eyes studying him. "I've seen that face before," he said. "I don't know where, but I'm sure I've seen him."

"Come on, bud," the guard told Alan. "You're going to answer some questions downstairs." He led Alan back toward the door.

Wrenching his arms free, Alan ran back toward the horseshoe-shaped table. The eyes of the ministers of all the federated Earth states were on him. He took a deep breath and said, "Gentlemen, I am Alan Tremaine."

CHAPTER SEVEN

ALAN remembered only vaguely what happened then. Sidearms were whipped out by the guards. One dignified member of the Council lunged across the table, dignity forgotten, and tried to slap Alan. The reporters, sensing something important when Alan had broken away from the guards downstairs and plunged inside the White House, had entered the room. Now the television cameras were grinding. There was not a friendly face in the room.

"Listen to me!" Alan shouted. He could not make himself heard over the babble of excitement in the room. He pounded on the table, and cried, "You've got to listen! Do you think I came here to die with all of you and all Earth tomorrow night? Do you?"

The guards held him again, one of them wrenching his right arm up and back painfully. The members of the Security Council were grim-lipped and silent. One of them restrained the Minister from France, who was still trying to get at Alan. "You...you are the worst traitor since Judas Iscariot," the Minister from France told Alan.

"I never sent that ultimatum," Alan shouted. "I wouldn't be here if I did. Are you going to listen to me?"

There was an angry murmuring from the horseshoe-shaped table. A reporter broke away from his companions and swung his fist awkwardly at Alan's face. "You have that coming," he said, "from five billion Earthmen."

Even the members of the Council seemed to approve. Some of them stood up and came around the table toward

Alan menacingly. Laura's words screamed inside Alan's skull—*they'll kill you*.

"Stop!" President Holland's firm voice boomed across the room. "Are we all animals here? Tremaine has the right to speak. With the Earth about to die, are we not even going to clutch at straws? Tremaine knows we can keep him here until tomorrow night, yet he came. I want to hear him. I will hear him if I have to do it alone."

The Ministers assumed their places at the table sheepishly. The television cameras panned closer to Alan. He could sense it: five billion people were watching him.

He talked rapidly. He didn't know how long they would listen. He told them how he had gone to Mars to take his father's place, told them how Richard Tremaine, then Eugene Talbrick had been murdered in cold blood by Bennett Keifer because he favored violence and complete dissolution of the union and they did not. He told them how Keifer still intended to use the name of Tremaine because Alan's father had been loved by the Outworlders and respected by the government of Earth. He told them how General Olmstead had been taken and eventually killed. They were listening now. Still doubtful, but listening. He could sense that some of the hostility had gone from them. They were weary now, and without hope in their eyes.

He went on, "I still think more than half the Outworlders would rally behind me. Maybe I don't deserve their faith, but they remember my father who spent his whole life and finally died in their cause. Let them know I'm here. Beam it to the Outworlds. Tell them I renounce Keifer as a traitor to his own people and to the Earth that spawned them. I'll talk if you want. I'll go on the air."

"Fool!" cried the Minister from France bitterly. "Even if it would work, what does it matter? Tomorrow we all die."

"There's a chance you won't," Alan said. "I'm coming to that. To bring you up to date, I landed on Earth a few hours ago and left General Olmstead's daughter with a friend at the PBT Fraternity House of New Washington University. You can check everything I said with her."

"You said there was a chance?"

"Yes. When did Keifer give his ultimatum?"

"Forty eight hours ago."

"That's what I figured. Unless the cobalt bomb was on its way to Earth for at least eight or ten days, it couldn't reach here from Mars or Venus by tomorrow night!"

"Then you mean it's all a bluff?" the Secretary General demanded, hope springing into his eyes.

"NO," Alan admitted. "It's no bluff. Two weeks ago, Keifer shut the flow of water through the space-warp from Venus to Mars. Now I realize why. He did it partly to get the people of Mars behind him when he issued his own ultimatum. He didn't want a revolution on his hands. But he did it for another reason, too.

"Gentlemen, if you know your astronomy, you'd know that a fairly rare astronomical event has happened. Venus, Earth and Mars are all in conjunction on the same side of the sun. To put it another way, Venus, with the shortest, fastest orbit, has overtaken the Earth's orbital position with respect to the sun. That's known as the synodic year. Earth has likewise overtaken slower Mars, so the three planets are lined up…"

"Imbecile!" screamed the Minister from France. "Here you stand, giving us astronomical puzzles, while Earth hovers on the brink of disaster."

"It's important," Alan said patiently. "Venus, Earth and Mars are in a line right now. Venus and Earth separated by some twenty-eight million miles. Earth and Mars by less than forty million. What I'm saying is this: Keifer didn't block Venusian water from the space-warp merely to rally the Outworlders behind him when he claimed you were responsible. He did it because the space-warp now passes within a couple of hundred thousand miles from Earth. He did it because he intends to transport the cobalt bomb here through the space-warp. I say that's the only way he can get it here in time..."

President Holland stood up, his face white, excitement in his eyes. "Yes," he said. "Yes, it's possible. We'll check the data with the New Washington Naval Observatory at once. If what you say is true, Tremaine...

"It almost has to be true, sir," Alan replied. "Keifer will need a launching site for his cobalt bomb after he takes it from the space-warp, but I have a hunch you'll find when you call the observatory that the moon's orbital position at this time passes within a few hundred miles of the space-warp. I say Keifer will launch his cobalt bomb at the Earth from the moon."

Now the reporters, suddenly friendly, were asking Alan so many questions that President Holland had to drag Alan away from them. A special jet took Alan, the President and a few advisors to the Naval Observatory, where Alan's, theory was confirmed. One of the astronomers told President Holland jubilantly, "All you have to do is send a fleet out to where the space warp intersects the orbit of the moon and..."

"How can we?" President Holland groaned. "We've dispatched almost all our ships to Mars, Venus and the Jovian moons to help put down the Outworld insurrections. We're left with a few obsolete, ancient ships."

"It doesn't matter," Alan said. "Keifer's in the same boat. His own ships have to defend the Outworlds. He'll only have a small fleet there, if any. He's depending on surprise, don't you see? Even if your ships couldn't get through, I'd have a chance. I'm Alan Tremaine. Tremaine. The Outworlders still think I'm in charge. They'll, have to let me through."

"You'll leave at once," President Holland told him. "In the three hours since you've been here, Alan Tremaine, you've given us new hope." He placed his hand on Alan's shoulder, looking at him long and searchingly. "All Earth must put its hope in you now. We don't have time to check your story thoroughly. We can't. Tremaine, never did so many people put their fate so completely in one man's hands as all Earth is putting its fate in yours. If you're lying, if you're telling the truth but wrong in your theory, life on Earth perishes. All life, Tremaine."

"I've got to be right, sir," Alan told the President. "I've got to."

President Holland smiled. "I'm tired, Tremaine. We're all tired, but we've got to go on. What ships we have will be ready to leave in an hour."

An hour, Alan thought. Now was the time to say goodbye to Laura. Now, with Earth solidly behind him. Now he could tell her of his hopes for the future, which did not seem so bleak. He must see her before he blasted off for the final reckoning with Keifer.

NO sounds came from the fraternity house in New Washington University. He called Bill Graham's name, but heard nothing. "Laura?" he said. "Laura, where are you?" The place seemed completely deserted.

"Alan Tremaine, is that you?" He whirled—and grinned. Mrs. Moriarity, the fraternity Rouse mother, stood below him on the stairs.

"I thought I recognized your voice young man. My hearing isn't so good anymore."

"Where's Bill Graham?"

"Upstairs, I suppose. He had some visitors before, Alan. Two men. I...I didn't like them. I didn't think Bill would have such friends. And Alan, they came downstairs with a lady. A woman! She must have been in Bill's room. There was an awful rumpus up there, then they came down. I'm going to give Bill Graham a talking to, you can bet."

Alan rushed upstairs without answering. Mrs. Moriarity was still talking, her voice carrying up from below. "How did you like your trip to Mars, Alan? I meant to ask you." Her own small world went on. The bigger world hadn't mattered for years, still didn't matter, even now.

Bill Graham's room was a shambles. Furniture turned over, the desk on its side, the bed...

Graham was on the floor. He lay with his hands in front of his face. His final gesture had been an instinctive one of protection. Half his face had been sheared away horribly by an atomic blast.

Laura was gone.

Final reckoning with Keifer, Alan thought. Bill Graham. Happy-go-lucky. A big kid who hadn't quite grown up yet. Give you the shirt off his back. Now he was dead.

How? Alan thought of it briefly and vaguely. It hardly mattered. It seemed impossible, too—but other things were more important. Except for Graham and Alan, only the reporters, guards and Ministers at the Security Council meeting had known where Laura was. Alan had told them.

There was a traitor among them.

The traitor had come here and taken Laura, killing Graham when he tried to prevent it.

Laura was bound for the moon. Keifer's final trump card.

Alan shook his fist impotently, then slammed it down on the overturned desk. *I'm coming, Laura,* he thought.

I'm coming, Bennett Keifer.

CHAPTER EIGHT

"SIX ships," President Holland told Alan at the New Washington Spaceport. "That's all we could make ready in time, Tremaine. Six battered line ships, out of commission for five years. It's all we had."

"I'm sorry, sir," a man in the uniform of a four star general told the President. "We sent all our power to the Outworlds."

"You couldn't do anything else, General," President Holland said. "We had received no ultimatum then. It seemed incredible Keifer or anyone would dare attack the Earth."

"I'll get through," Alan said. Flood lights stabbed out across the dark field, criss-crossing it with brilliant beams of light. Ground crews scurried like insects caught in their glare, fueling the six spaceships, checking them, trying to accomplish an extensive reconditioning job in minutes.

Soon the spacecrews were jogging out on the field in bulky blast suits, small gleaming figures in the light of the floods. On one of the ships Alan saw the blue and gold symbol of the Outworld Federation, freshly painted, side by side with the globe and stars of Earth.

"You're blasting off for the good people of the Federation as well as for the Earth," President Holland explained. "We've radioed the Outworlds and told them. We don't know the effect, if any."

"Keifer will have his hands full," Alan said. "I hope…"

The jogging figures of the spacemen had separated into six groups of half a dozen men each, one group for each of the battered old ships.

"There's a launching site at the old, abandoned Terra Mines in Tycho Crater on the moon," President Holland told Alan. "If you don't get Keifer at the space-warp and stop him there, you'll probably find him in Tycho."

President Holland and the four star general were walking across the dark field with Alan now, toward the lead ship, standing on its tail in the glare of the floodlights. "All Earth is blasting off with you, Tremaine," the President said.

He shook hands solemnly with Alan. So did the General. Alan closed the airlock door behind him, heard a plopping sound as the airtight rubberoid fabric of the circular door gripped the hull and sealed it. The spacemen were at their stations, not talking, not smoking. Waiting.

Through the viewport, Alan watched President Holland and the General trotting out of the blast-off area.

Alan walked into the control room, past the grim, silent crew, each man stationed at his obsolete equipment. Half a dozen overage ships, with Earth's fate in the balance.

And Laura up there somewhere.

"Let's go," Alan said.

The rocket engines whined and shrieked into life. Alan and the pilot strapped themselves into blast chairs. The roar was deafening. Alan could feel his face contorted by eight G's pressure as the ancient spaceship blasted off. Then his muscles bunched in agony, he blacked out.

DAZZLING white with reflected sunlight but pock-marked with craters, shadowed with deep valleys and gorges, sundered by great rock faults, puckered with vast bleak mountain ranges, the moon swept up at them.

"That reporter wants to see you now, Mr. Tremaine," the pilot told Alan.

"I haven't time for—what? What reporter?"

"The one President Holland sent along to cover the story for Earth."

"He didn't tell me—" Alan began, then shrugged. The reporter would be a nuisance, but it hardly mattered. "No interviews now," Alan said. "Tell him we're not going to land on the moon—yet. Tell him we're looking for the space warp."

Gem-bright, unblinking, the stars of space gleamed through the viewport. Star-maps were spread on the floor of the small control cabin, crewmembers pouring over them. Somewhere out there, space should look different. Somewhere, starlight should be cut off by a narrow band of blackness—the space-warp. They had to find it, and they had to hurry. It made good sense to tell the Outworlders Alan had denounced Bennett Keifer as a traitor, for some of them might not fire on Alan's six small ships. But it also presented a danger: Keifer would probably abandon the hour of his ultimatum and rush ahead with his plans. They had mere minutes to find the space-warp. Perhaps already it was too late.

With the pilot taking over, Alan kneeled on the floor and studied the star-maps, calling out grid-coordinates while a man at the viewports checked them against space itself. Soon his head was swimming with the multitudes of white dots on the blueprint paper, with the white graph lines, the swarms of stars. "Sixteen-eleven," he said. "Deneb, Vega, Altair... Sixteen, twelve, Pollux, Procyon, Sirius..."

"Check...check..."

"Seventeen, one, Achernar, Canopus..."

"Check..."

Check, *check*, CHECK!

"Nineteen, three, Capella, Regulus, Alpha Centauri... Nineteen, four..."

"Hold it! Wait a minute, Mr. Tremaine. If you draw a line from Capella through Regulus to Centauri, what else should you cross?"

Alan looked at his map. "You come close to Castor and Pollux, close to Cancer; you cross the constellations Crater and Corvus."

"Not out here, you don't."

Then Alan was running to the viewport. Between bright, unblinking Regulus and even brighter Alpha Centauri was— nothing. A hole in space. A long, narrow path of intense, unbroken blackness.

"That's it!" Alan nearly shouted. He felt like laughing, like pounding the man's back, like dancing a jig. They had found the space warp.

Alan ran to the pilot chair, swinging the small ship around almost ninety degrees. In the rear viewscreen he could see the five other ships wheeling about and following.

And something else—in front of them. Specks moving across the firmament in tight formation, growing.

Keifer's fleet.

HE counted fifteen ships, each larger and with more firepower than his own, guardians of the space-warp, rocketing down toward them from where Corvus should have been, from the hole in space behind which the constellation Crater hid.

Alan flicked his radio toggle to the on position, said into it: "This is Alan Tremaine calling the Outworld fleet. Tremaine calling! Do you hear me?"

"Go back to Earth, Tremaine. We don't want to kill you."

"I'm flying the flags of Earth and the Federation. If you listen to me, it still isn't too late for Equal Union. I denounce

Bennett Keifer as a traitor to Earth and the Outworld Federation, as my father would have done."

"Go back to Earth, Tremaine."

Alan shook his head, then scrambled the radio frequency to his small fleet's band. "Flagship calling," he said. "We're heading for the warp. Hold off the Federation fleet at all costs."

And, to the pilot: "Take her in, Stan. I'm getting into spacegear."

Five obsolete ships against the Federation's bigger fleet. A sixth ship to reach the warp and hover there while Alan explored. The odds against them seemed tremendous, but Alan brushed them from his mind. Swiftly, he climbed into a bulky spacesuit, inflating it while one of the crew secured the glassite helmet over his head. He tested the suit radio, secured a set of personnel jets to his shoulders, then clomped into the airlock with an atomic rifle, slamming the ammo pan into place in the breech. He stood impatiently at the outer door of the airlock, looking through the small viewport into space. Spinning in a great wheel formation, the three-dimensional equivalent of the ancient naval maneuver called crossing the T, the Federation fleet spun toward them.

Out to meet it—five ships, darting like silver midges at the giant wheel.

All at once, energy erupted searingly before his eyes as the fleets met. Two ships in the Federation wheel darkened and fell, tumbling end over end, out of rank. But one Earth ship was blown to pieces. If the rate of attrition continued...

He didn't think about it. He spun the mechanism that controlled the outer airlock door and pulled himself out on the hull of the ship. The battle formations were drifting behind him now. Ahead the black tube of the space-warp.

Pointing himself toward the blackness, Alan fired his shoulder jets.

HERE along the vast track of the warp, a station hung in space. As it swelled up toward him, Alan could make out three tiny figures, three men in spacesuits, watching him.

Space erupted violently about him as two of the figures raised atomic rifles to their shoulders and fired. Switching his jets on and off, Alan darted erratically through space to present a difficult target.

He was a hundred yards from the warp-station now. Overhead, his flagship was hovering on the sunward side of the station, casting a huge black shadow across it. Aiming carefully, Alan fired his own atomic rifle.

One of the figures collapsed on the surface of the station. The second was still firing at him. The third, unarmed, was watching. Alan swung quickly around to the dark side of the small globe, strapped the rifle to his shoulders, alighted on his hands, and cartwheeled upright. Without pausing for breath, he unstrapped the rifle, held it ready at his hip and sprinted around the station.

Two heads bobbed into view on the incredibly close horizon. Tremaine and the Federation soldier fired simultaneously. Alan could feel the heat of the blast through his spacesuit. Before his eyes, his glassite helmet fused. A bare slit remained for him to see through.

But the second Federation soldier had fallen.

"I'm unarmed!" the third man screamed over his suit radio.

Alan recognized Captain—no, *Major*—Haddix's voice. "Lead me to the warp, Haddix," he said. "No tricks."

Seconds later, Alan was following the spacesuited figure across the smooth black surface of the warp-station. He passed one of the fallen soldiers, a gash torn in the fabric of his spacesuit. The body and head had swelled horribly against the suddenly unequal pressure. The thing inside the suit did not look human.

Haddix stopped at the brink of the space-warp, waiting for Alan with his back to the pit.

"Has the bomb come through yet?" Alan demanded.

Haddix made a lewd gesture, but his face paled behind the glassite helmet when Alan raised the atomic rifle and calmly began squeezing the trigger.

"Wait! I'll tell you. Don't point that thing..."

"Talk, damn you."

"It's already on the moon, Tremaine. Keifer changed his plans when he knew you were coming. But take it from me, you don't have a chance."

"What about General Olmstead's daughter?"

"She's with him, I think. Listen, Tremaine. Go easy. I'm only a professional soldier. I do what I'm told."

At that moment, a second shadow darted across the surface of the warp-station. Instinctively, Alan looked up. A Federation ship had come to do battle with the Earth ship hovering there, flashing by it and unleashing a salvo of raw energy. The Earth ship was swinging around to bring its own atomics to bear...

And then Haddix was upon him, clawing for the atomic rifle. They struggled there at the lip of the space-warp, the weapon between them. Slowly, Alan felt himself being forced around, felt nothing but space below his left foot as he tried to step back. Immediately behind him was the warp, and instant, horrible death if he fell in.

Haddix's gauntleted fist struck his glassite helmet, jarring him. Alan swung both of his arms wildly for balance, then remembered his personnel jets and switched them on, pivoting around at the same instant. Borne aloft by his shoulder rockets, Alan and Haddix spun dizzily over the abyss.

It was Haddix's own blind fury that killed him.

He swung his fists at Alan, trying to shatter the already damaged glassite helmet. In the heat of battle he forgot that Alan alone wore the jets.

Alan watched the figure tumbling below him, head over heels, slowly, as in a dream. Haddix's voice came to him once over the radio in a blaring, hideous scream. Then the spacesuited form was swept into the warp, where it twisted, was bent, and broken...

Overhead, the Earth ship hovered. Far away, the gutted hulk of the Federation craft, which had come to challenge it, was drifting off into space. Alan jetted for the Earth ship.

HANDS lifted the helmet from his head, deflated and unfastened the spacesuit. "How are the others making out?" Alan gasped.

"They're gone. All gone. Five ships, five brave crews..."

"And the Federation?"

"Three ships left."

"Can we beat them to the moon?"

"We can try."

Just then the reporter joined Alan and the two crewmen in the companionway. "You'll reach the moon, all right," he said.

He was pointing an atomic pistol at them.

CHAPTER NINE

COLD and lifeless, the surface of the moon expanded before them. The six-man crew of the spaceship sat in the control cabin. Alan was at the controls. The reporter stood at the door, facing them with his back to the companionway. The atomic pistol was unwavering in his hand.

"You were at the Security Council meeting," Alan said bitterly. "You're working for Keifer. You sent those men to kidnap Laura. Then, in the confusion at the space field, you claimed the President had designated you to cover the story for Earth, and—"

The reporter nodded. "A man's a fool not to join the winning side while he can. You'll take this ship down in Tycho crater. You'll land near the old Terra Mines dome. They'll drag you in through the domelock with a tractor beam. You'll be able to watch them launch the bomb to Earth."

Jagged, pockmarked, and buried in its mantle of pumice, the surface of the moon sped by below them. Dark and somber, the broad deep valleys of the moon, appeared, were reached, and then left behind. Rills cut tortuously across the moonscape; rays like molten gold radiated from some of the craters.

Finally, the great ringwall of Tycho crater flashed into view. At one side, just inside the ringwall of the crater and more than two-score miles from the lonely central peaks, the glassite dome that had housed Terra Mines in the early days of space travel could be seen.

Alan brought the spaceship down on its tail, its rocket exhaust blasting the pumice below with blistering heat.

There was still time, Alan thought.

But they were helpless.

He wondered if, in decisive moments, history was full of such traitors—men like the reporter who would soon bring civilization on Earth, life on Earth, to an end when he returned Alan and his crew over to Keifer's Federation forces within the dome. He shrugged—then wondered also how strongly a man had to believe to forfeit his life for a principle.

For if he tried anything, the reporter would kill him.

If he didn't, you could count the time remaining for Earth in hours.

Abruptly, he slapped his hand across the firing lever, heard the surge of sudden power at the same moment that the ship rocked and plunged moonward on its side. There were shouts behind him in the cabin. There was a split-second of confusion.

Alan spun around and dove across the room for the reporter. The man had fallen and was just climbing to his feet when Alan reached him. He must have decided there was no time to fire. Instead, he hurled the heavy weapon at Alan.

It struck his shoulder then fell away. Then he was on the reporter, reaching for his throat, choking him, strangling... Hands dragged him clear.

"He's unconscious," someone said. "Layoff, Tremaine."

There was a lurch as tractor beams from the dome caught and held the spaceship. They were tugged through the domelock but all were heavily armed with atomic rifles and pistols when the ship came to a stop inside.

ANOTHER ship lay on its side within the half-mile-in-diameter dome. A dozen men stood about, waiting for them to be delivered like sheep.

Alan led his men outside into the cool, canned air of the dome. Their concentrated fire was unexpected and deadly, dropping the Federation men where they stood. Three or four of them managed to crawl behind the second ship, from where they returned the fire. One of Alan's men fell.

"Quick!" Alan cried. "Three of you cut around the front of the ship. Stan and I will slip around the tail rockets."

Without waiting for an answer, he led the pilot through a fierce barrage of atomic pellets toward the rear of the spaceship. As the missiles struck the ground on all sides of them, they exploded violently, kicking up man-tall geysers of Luna pumice.

"You're covered from both sides!" Alan shouted, poking his head cautiously around the rocket tubes. His answer was a stream of atomic pellets, which struck the tubes and fused them. Ignoring the deadly fire, Alan plunged on, feeling the kick of his own atomic rifle as he triggered shot after shot blindly ahead of him.

There were two men left alive back there, standing back to back, trembling, their hands high over their heads.

"Where's Keifer?" Alan barked at them.

One pointed vaguely outside the dome. "The central mountains," he said.

"What are you talking about?"

"A shipload of technicians brought the bomb there from the space-warp. That's where Terra Mines had its launching equipment. Honest. I swear it's the truth."

"Is Keifer there too?"

"Yes. With the girl. They went out in one of Terra Mines' old Luna tanks to watch the launching."

"When is it?"

"Half an hour, maybe less," the Federation soldier said. "You couldn't stop them. You'll never get there in time."

"Is there another tank?"

The soldier nodded, pointed across the pumice to a squat green vehicle with caterpillar treads. Alan was already running for it and calling over his shoulder. "Stay here. If the remaining Federation ships try to come down, use the dome-guns on them. Stan, you come with me."

The pilot sprinted after him. Together they entered the moon tank, which was not airtight. They found Terra Mines spacesuits inside, the ancient, long-unused type that looked like deep sea suits. The tank's rocket engine sputtered and caught. The tank lumbered toward the domelock and through it while they donned the spacesuits.

Then they were bouncing soundlessly across the airless surface of Tycho crater, leaving the dome far behind them. Earth was above them in the sky, in the quarter-phase. You could see part of North America reflecting sunlight. Blue-black, the Pacific Ocean was in shadow.

Ahead loomed the central mountains of Tycho crater, biting into the black sky, saw-toothed, for fifteen thousand feet. On labored the moon tank, climbing now, its old engine whining a protest against the steep grade, the sound echoing strangely inside the vehicle because outside in the Luna vacuum it could not be heard at all. They crossed the first peak of the range, looked down on a great cauldron in the rock, a crater within the crater, a mile across.

At one end was a Federation spaceship, standing on its tail rockets and pointing up at the sky like a gleaming needle.

At the other end was the launching platform, massive, indistinct in the gloomy shadows of the mountains. On the platform, partially out of shadow, rested the cobalt bomb, big as a small spaceship.

Another tank sped toward them across the uneven moonscape. Two men were perched atop it in red spacesuits, firing already although they were still out of range.

ALAN tapped Stan on the shoulder and told the pilot he was going outside. He slipped through the hatch and climbed on top of the lurching tank, squatting there and slamming a fresh ammo pan into his atomic rifle.

The trip across the crater had consumed ten minutes of the time left for Earth. What remained—twenty minutes? Twenty-five?

Suddenly, the moon tank shuddered beneath Alan's feet. They had come within range sooner than he had expected. He felt himself hurled away, and tumbled across the rocks as the tank burst briefly into flame, devouring in seconds the oxygen stored in the fuel tanks. With an eerie, noiseless blast, the tank exploded.

Alan scrambled forward across the rocks. Somehow, he had managed to hold his atomic rifle. He wondered if the mechanism had been damaged by his fall.

He didn't have time to think about it. The other tank, now less than fifty yards away, was coming toward him. He fired once, forced to reveal his position. A spacesuited figure fell from the tank, but another climbed up through the hatch to join the man still kneeling there.

The tank was thirty yards away now, still coming.

Concealed partially behind an outcropping of rock, Alan fired again, saw a second figure tumble off the roof of the tank, rolling down a steep incline. The third man was returning his fire, but wildly. At the last moment he tried to scramble within the hatch, but his glassite helmet exploded as one of Alan's pellets caught it.

The tank was upon him, its caterpillar treads rolling soundlessly across the rock. Flinging his rifle out of the way,

Alan dove between the two great treads and clung there. He could feel the jagged rocks cutting into his spacesuit, scraping it, weakening the fabric. In seconds, the fabric would rupture.

There was a hatch on the underbelly of the tank. Dragged along, Alan held on with one hand and pried at the hatch with the other. He was bruised and shaken by the rocks.

The hatch swung clear.

Alan chinned himself into the tank. A spacesuited figure sat over the controls. Another one was staring at Alan through the glassite helmet of a modern spacesuit.

It was Laura.

He didn't know if she would recognize him through the visor of his ancient suit. She screamed, "Alan! Look out!"

Keifer was rising from the controls, plunging toward him. Alan met him half way over the open hatch, grappling with him there. In Keifer's hand was an atomic pistol. He couldn't bring it down to bear on Alan, but was beating him across the head with it, the sound of metal striking metal booming in Alan's ears. If his helmet had been glassite, he thought, Keifer could have killed him.

Alan lost his footing and slipped, spread-eagling over the open hatch. Keifer fell on him, pushing, trying to force him through. "You can't stop the bomb," he said, his voice cold and metallic over the suit radio. "It's all automatic now."

For answer, Alan swung his metal-shod fists at Keifer's glassite helmet. He felt himself slipping. In seconds, Keifer's weight would drive him through the hatch. He pounded the glassite helmet above him. Blindly, he kept on pounding it. His legs were slipping, dangling through the hatch over the jagged rocks. The slightest rip in the fabric of his suit would bring instant death.

All at once, a crack appeared in Keifer's helmet, running from crown to chin. Alan struck again with his right fist.

The crack became a hole. Keifer opened his mouth to scream, but then his face was swelling, bloated—became a shapeless thing that no longer could fit within the helmet.

Trembling, Alan stood up and rushed to the control. He saw that Laura was already heading the moon tank back toward the launching platform. He had a few seconds in which to play.

The tank lurched to a stop beside the platform.

HAND over hand, Alan was climbing the scaffold. He reached the platform with the tank's atomic rifle strapped across his shoulders. Half a dozen technicians were preparing to leave.

"Shut it off!" Alan shouted. "Don't launch that bomb!"

"We can't stop it now. The mechanism is set."

"I'll kill you if I have to."

"We can't, don't you understand? The bomb will be launched in five minutes—no, four minutes and fifty seconds now. Once set, it's fully automatic. We didn't want to set it. Keifer made us do it. You're Alan Tremaine, aren't you?" the technician asked. "We're on your side, Tremaine. Most of the Outworlds are, ever since Earth's broadcast. But Keifer came here with a hard core of his followers in a small fleet and—"

"Never mind the talk. Can't you render the bomb harmless?"

The technician shook his head within the glassite helmet.

Overhead, the quarter-phase Earth was shining brightly, waiting helplessly.

"It's the radioactive cobalt that will do the damage," Alan said. "An atomic trigger for the hydrogen bomb, a hydrogen trigger for the cobalt, right?"

"Essentially, yes."

"Then strip off the cobalt, you fools!"

"Three minutes," someone said. "We've got to get out of here. The after-burners of the launching charge will cremate us."

"It can be done," one of the technicians told Alan, "but I don't think you have the time."

"How, man? Tell me how!"

"Use your rifle. There's a seam running around the bomb. See? See it? If you can cut around the whole seam, the cobalt should fall away in two hemispheres. A hydrogen bomb alone would be launched at Earth, but it should fall harmlessly into the Pacific Ocean."

"Two minutes, forty seconds."

The technicians moved about uneasily. Two of them began to climb down the scaffold. The rest remained to watch Alan. They would save the Earth or perish with him.

Alan raised his atomic rifle to his shoulder, aimed at the thin welded seam about the huge bomb, and began to fire. At first there was nothing. The pellets hit the bomb, which could only be triggered by an atomic implosion at its core, and exploded there.

"A minute and a half," someone said, his voice hoarse over Alan's suit radio.

The seam was widening, became a gap a foot across. Alan continued firing, the rifle slapping back against his numb shoulder. The crack spread around the circumference of the bomb.

"One minute to blast-off!"

Alan fired his last volley, stood there in despair. He had run out of ammunition.

The cobalt outer skin of the bomb shook, spread apart, fell away in two equal hemispheres. The technicians were plunging down the scaffold, Alan right behind them. They tumbled inside the moon tank.

Laura didn't have to be told. The tank bounced away at full speed.

Behind them, a brilliant flash lit the lunar sky. For a moment, Alan could see the hydrogen bomb streaking Earthward, a silver speck against the blackness. Then it was gone. It was a vast trigger now, and nothing more. Harmlessly, it would explode in the Pacific Ocean, like dozens of tests that had been conducted there.

The Outworlds would agree to Equal Union now. Alan knew that. The technician had told him. They had never liked the war. They were ready to rally behind his name. There would be some ugliness between Earth and the Outworlds for a time, because of what had almost happened. But it would pass.

The Lunar Mines dome loomed ahead of them. The dome-lock opened to admit them.

"I wish we were inside already," Laura said, "where there's some air."

"What for?" Alan asked her.

"So I can take off this helmet and kiss you."

Nothing would suit Alan better. Now, at last, they were inside. He took off his helmet.

THE END

If you've enjoyed this book, you will not want to miss these terrific titles...

ARMCHAIR SCI-FI & HORROR DOUBLE NOVELS, $12.95 each

D-121 **THE GENIUS BEASTS** by Frederik Pohl
THIS WORLD IS TABOO by Murray Leinster

D-122 **THE COSMIC LOOTERS** by Edmond Hamilton
WANDL THE INVADER by Ray Cummings

D-123 **ROBOT MEN OF BUBBLE CITY** by Rog Phillips
DRAGON ARMY by William Morrison

D-124 **LAND BEYOND THE LENS** by S. J. Byrne
DIPLOMAT-AT-ARMS by Keith Laumer

D-125 **VOYAGE OF THE ASTEROID, THE** by Laurence Manning
REVOLT OF THE OUTWORLDS by Milton Lesser

D-126 **OUTLAW IN THE SKY** by Chester S. Geier
LEGACY FROM MARS by Raymond Z. Gallun

D-127 **THE GREAT FLYING SAUCER INVASION** by Geoff St. Reynard
THE BIG TIME by Fritz Leiber

D-128 **MIRAGE FOR PLANET X** by Stanley Mullen
POLICE YOUR PLANET by Lester del Rey

D-129 **THE BRAIN SINNERS** by Alan E. Nourse
DEATH FROM THE SKIES by A. Hyatt Verrill

D-139 **CRY CHAOS** by Dwight V. Swain
THE DOOR THROUGH SPACE By Marion Zimmer Bradley

ARMCHAIR SCIENCE FICTION CLASSICS, $12.95 each

C-55 **UNDER THE TRIPLE SUNS**
by Stanton A. Coblentz

C-56 **STONE FROM THE GREEN STAR**
by Jack Williamson

C-57 **ALIEN MINDS**
by E. Everett Evans

ARMCHAIR MASTERS OF SCIENCE FICTION SERIES, $16.95 each

G-13 **SCIENCE FICTION GEMS, Vol. Seven**
Jack Vance and others

G-14 **HORROR GEMS, Vol. Seven**
Robert Bloch and others